Standing Room

Standing Room

STORIES BY
HOLLIS SUMMERS

Louisiana State University Press
Baton Rouge & London   1984

Designer: Barbara Werden
Typeface: Linotron Primer
Typesetter: G & S Typesetters, Inc.
Printer and binder: Edwards Brothers, Inc.

Library of Congress Cataloging in Publication Data

Summers, Hollis Spurgeon, 1916–
Standing room.

Contents: Herschell—Amaryllis and the telephone—
A hundred paths—[etc.]
I. Title.
PS3537.U72S78   1984   813'.54   84-10004
ISBN 0-8071-1191-0
ISBN 0-8071-1200-3 (pbk.)

In earlier versions some of the stories in this collection have appeared in the following publications and are reprinted with their permission: *Colorado Quarterly, Epoch, Perspective, San Francisco Review.* "The Vireo's Nest" is reprinted from *Prairie Schooner*, by permission of University of Nebraska Press. Copyright © 1960 University of Nebraska Press.

For Bea and William

Contents

Standing Room

Herschell

I COME from old Kentucky families.
    I have been told since I was old enough to listen that I come from old families, my father's family, the Baxters, with a land grant in 1799; my mother's, the Archers, in 1832. Mother never forgave the Baxters for their earlier arrival.

"They were farmers. They worked other people's lands after they lost their own," Mother said and said. "But they were God-fearing people. There's nothing to be ashamed of in your father's lineage. It's just that he never took any interest in his forebears. I must admit, Archie Lee, I consider that a character flaw. But I'm not speaking against your father. I've never spoken against him. Isn't that true, Archie?"

"Yeah. Sure," I said and said, not wanting the conversation to continue.

The Archers were professional people, ministers, professors, lawyers, even a judge. "But you aren't to be vain about your inheritance on my side. Inheritance, like grace, is something we don't deserve. It's something to thank God for, but quietly."

The portrait of Great Great Great Grandmother Phoebe Essex is my earliest memory. Always, in the variously miserable houses we rented through my youth, Grandmother stood above a fireplace, over a couch, between windows, watching me. She is a young girl with an old woman's face. Her hands rest on a pedestal. Her background is blue and gray fog. She is contained within a frame of gold curlicues bumping into each other. Beneath her is a museum light. Every dusk of my life in those rented houses Mother turned on the light under Grandmother Phoebe's picture. The last person to bed was supposed to turn Grandmother out.

"Have you turned Grandmother out?" Mother called from her bedroom.

More often than I fumbled down dark stairs to make sure the water heater was turned off I went to check on Grandmother Phoebe.

Grandmother seemed to look at me, even after the light was out. It was only a trick of the moon or a streetlight, a trick of twelve-year-old eyes, my twenty-one-year-old eyes, twenty-five, the eyes of a man who lived in a house with his mother for thirty-five years.

As a child I often studied the picture. I stood on a chair to look at her. I lay with my head hanging over the edge of a couch, making the world upside down, imagining the light fixture a candelabra on the white floor of the ceiling, Grandmother and her pedestal standing on their heads.

There was something wrong with Grandmother from every angle.

Her right arm and hand were good enough, but her left arm didn't belong to her body. The left arm wasn't long enough to reach the pedestal, but it reached the pedestal.

I worried about Grandmother. Perhaps, with her young body and her old face, she was a dwarf. Perhaps she was painfully crippled. Perhaps I would inherit her body. Maybe I would never grow tall enough to be a man. Maybe my arm, my right arm—inheritances changed from women to men—would be so crippled I could never catch a baseball. Often, looking at her, I clenched my fists, imagining baseballs. It did not once enter my mind to ask Mother about Grandmother Phoebe's deformity.

MOTHER never encouraged me to learn to fix, to mend or repair. I think she wanted to spare my hands, as if she nurtured Paderewski, Kreisler, Rodin. Mr. Barnes, my friend Herschell's father, was our handyman. Mother called on Mr. Barnes for everything from light switches to leaking faucets.

God knows my hands were not worth saving for any reason except for the convenience of having hands. For a year I studied violin with Mrs. Keeton next door in exchange for Mother's taking care of the Keeton twins twice a week. During fourth grade, after my father's death, I studied the piano. Mother took great pride in saying, "Arch is studying the piano now." There was a year of oboe with Mr. Fontaine at the Normal School. I have no memory of how the piano or oboe lessons were paid for. I remember only the shame I felt when Mother boasted of my studies. Feeling I owed her something, I practiced hard. But I never made the junior orchestra or the junior band. In the seventh grade I took a paper route, not without a painful scene with Mother. She almost cried, but, being an Archer, she did not cry.

"Your music, Arch! Music is the soul of man. You'll thank me some day for your music. If you had a paper route you wouldn't have time for practicing."

I said, "You work too hard. I ought to be working. I thank you very much for my music. I thank you right now. Everybody has a paper route."

"*Everybody* being Herschell Barnes, I suppose."

"Yeah, he has one. But that's not the reason. And, anyhow, Herschell's my friend."

"Archer, I have told you and told you and told you . . ."

Mother fretted over my being able to have only one friend at a time.

"You should have a dozen friends, at least a dozen. Or more."

I told her, again, that I didn't want that many friends; I wouldn't know what to do with them. "There's nothing wrong with Herschell."

"I didn't say there was. Perhaps Mr. Barnes is a little . . . well, a little feckless."

I asked what *feckless* meant. I was learning three new words a day. Mother told me to never mind. "There's no reason in the world for you to take a paper route."

"Are you telling me I can't?"

We were standing in front of the mantel in the house on Elm Street.

I have not thought of that house in years.

That moment under Grandmother Phoebe's portrait was a moment of triumph for me, but I hardly relish remembering it.

Mother said, "You're thirteen."

I said, "I was just going to say I was thirteen."

I thought, "She's not as tall as she used to be. Or I'm getting taller." I said, "I'm not going to take oboe lessons any more."

Mother said, "Very well," and went back to the kitchen. I went upstairs and practiced at "The Stars and Stripes Forever" for almost an hour. By suppertime we were acting as if the day were just any old day.

THAT fall was as fine a season as I can remember. At school we were seated alphabetically. All day I sat by Herschell. After school we went straight to the *Messenger* office. Most days old Mr. Roberts was late in getting the paper out. We horsed around. We raced each other to the post office and back; we stole each other's caps. Herschell sang sometimes. When Herschell decided to sing everybody listened. He had learned the songs from an old Victrola his granddaddy had willed him. Herschell sang "O Sole Mio," and "Funiculi, Funicula," and "The Volga Boatman," and "Loch Lomond."

Herschell could do everything well. Herschell knew what he was going to do with his life. Miss Grange, our Sunday School teacher, said we all should know what we were going to do with our lives, but Herschell was the only one of us who really knew. He was going to be a radio singer. And then he was going to Hollywood and be a movie star. When he was about thirty years old he was coming back to Graham and buy Major Thompson's house at the edge of town, the house on the hill with porches that looked all over Scott County.

We never doubted Herschell's future. "We'll come to see you."

"Sure," Herschell said, even to the black kid who delivered the Buttermilk Lane route. "I'll be having a party every night or so. You're all invited."

I courted Herschell. I helped him with his arithmetic. While we were friends his grade in English changed from *D* to *A*. I imagined myself in a tuxedo entering Major Thompson's house on the hill. "Hello, old friend." Herschell was dressed in a white tuxedo. "My, but I'm glad to see you," Herschell said.

MONDAY'S *Messenger* was the lightest paper of the week. One Monday, it was October still, a red and yellow October that made you catch your breath, Herschell came home with me after we had delivered our papers. "We'll make popcorn," I promised. "Maybe we'll even have cider. And fresh apple cake, maybe."

Mother was cordial enough to Herschell, as cordial as she ever was. There was fresh apple cake, and cider. Every grain of the popcorn popped as complete as a snowflake.

We played three games of carom. Herschell won, even though it was difficult to make him win.

In the kitchen Mother rattled dishes and pans. I knew we were going to have soup and hamburgers. Soup and hamburgers shouldn't have made that much noise. I kept hoping Mother would ask Herschell to stay for supper.

At five-thirty Mother came into the living room to turn on Grandmother. Herschell leaned back in his chair. He slapped rhythmically at his stomach, making drum sounds. "Who in the world's that?" Herschell tossed his head, making his dark hair rise and fall.

"Phoebe Essex. You saw her before, that other time we played carom."

"Not with her light on. It don't look like anybody much."

"She's my three greats grandmother."

"What was the matter with her?"

Mother stood at the door to the dining room.

Herschell was my friend. I felt free to tell Herschell anything. I said, "She was crippled some way. I hope I don't catch it. I guess I won't, after all this time."

"I sure hope not."

"Archer Baxter!" Mother came into the living room, her hands on her hips. She looked like somebody angry in a comic strip. She was angry. "That is your great great great grandmother you are speaking of. She was not afflicted. She was a beautiful, cultured woman. All of the letters and diaries so attest."

Attest. It was a word I could add. I tried to think about the word.

Herschell said, "She looks crippled to me. She looks pretty bad off." Herschell always spoke up to everybody.

We were having a bad time, I remember—the grocery bill; we owed the dentist for my wisdom teeth; we had charged for my school clothes; maybe we still owed Herschell's father for fixing the electric iron and Mother's sewing machine. I thought about feeling sorry for Mother. But she need not have said, "She is *who* we are. Many people are uncertain of their own parentage."

I had no notion of what she was talking about. Herschell seemed to know. He was standing. He said, "I knowed Pa Tate. He left me his Victrola." He and Mother were looking hard at each other.

"Which is very nice," Mother said. "Archie has told me you have a splendid singing voice."

"I guess I better be gettin' home."

"It *is* late," Mother said. "I expect your family will be waiting for you. And, oh yes, Herschell. Would you mind asking Mr. Barnes to drop in some time tomorrow? The furnace. And the nights are getting cold. You'll be sure and tell *Mr.* Barnes."

"My daddy."

5

"Mr. Barnes."

"I guess I'll tell him."

"Herschell!"

"O.K. I'll tell him. But Pa Tate was a good singer. I got it from him. Singin'."

"I'm sure you do. Good-bye Herschell."

I said, "I'll walk you part of the way."

Mother said, "Supper's almost ready."

I walked with Herschell to the corner of Elm and Fourth Street. We did not talk.

I said, "I'll see you tomorrow."

"Sure." Herschell broke into a run. I thought of calling, "Last look." We were always calling, "Last Look," prolonging ourselves.

The soup that night was potato. The hamburger had gristle in it. I used the last of the mustard in the cut-glass jar. The milk was very cold.

I was ready to leave the table before I said, "I think you hurt Herschell's feelings. I don't know what you were talking about."

"There are certain subjects we do not discuss, Archie Lee."

"I got a right to know."

Mother said, "Evil communications corrupt good manners."

"I don't know what that means."

"I expect my son to be pure. The Barneses have values different from ours. Now, that's enough."

"For gosh sakes."

"That is a vulgar expression."

"Herschell's very nice. I don't know what you're talking about."

Mother said, "In the olden days itinerant artists visited country homes. They were not always master painters." She was making conversation as if I were company. "We are very fortunate that Grandmother Essex's portrait was done by a skilled craftsman. A number of years ago the museum in Cincinnati was quite interested in securing Grandmother for their permanent collection. I would not part with her."

"I know. I know that. What's the matter with Herschell?"

Mother patted her lips with her napkin. "You're excused, Arch. I'm sure you have homework to do. There's no need to help me with the dishes."

6

I didn't get to talk to Herschell at all the next day. While we were waiting for old man Roberts to bring out the *Messengers*, Herschell grabbed Eric Thompson's cap and raced him to the post office.

"How ya doing?" we kept asking each other.

THAT fall Herschell began working with his father, afternoons after school. Once—it was late December—Herschell came alone. The gas grate in my bedroom was broken.

I had had a terrible cold since Thanksgiving. Mother had insisted that I give up the paper route. I didn't mind giving it up.

I was glad to see Herschell. I stood in the doorway of my room and watched him. I dug my hands deep into the pockets of my corduroy pants. I was ashamed of my hands that couldn't play anything or fix anything.

Herschell hummed as he worked.

I said, "You tell me if I can help. Hold anything. Or anything?"

"I got it. It's coming all right."

I wanted to leave the doorway. I wished Mother would call me. She did not call.

I was coughing. I sounded like a dog barking.

Herschell said, "That's a pretty bad cough you got."

"Mother and I both have colds. I haven't been at school in a week."

"I thought I hadn't seen you around."

"I hope you don't catch anything from us."

Herschell laughed. "I never get a cold." He threw back his hair and smiled.

I said, "I hear Mother calling me. I got to go see what she wants." I hoped Herschell imagined he had heard Mother call. "You yell if I can do anything."

I was standing at the kitchen sink turning the water on and off when Herschell came downstairs. Mother was sewing in the dining room. I started to go up the back stairway. I changed my mind.

Mother was being polite to Herschell. "Now, you're sure you're charging me enough? I don't want to rob you."

"It wasn't anything very wrong. The valve. It was just clogged up."

I was in the dining room. Under Grandmother Phoebe's picture Mother was saying, "You must take this extra twenty cents. It means a great deal to me for Archie to be warm. I insist, Herschell."

7

I started to back into the kitchen. But Herschell was looking at me over Mother's shoulder. He didn't smile. Herschell dropped one of the dimes. Mother and Herschell and I looked at the dime's wobbling across the hearth. I imagined that it would never stop.

I walked over and picked up the dime and dropped it in Herschell's hand. Our hands did not touch.

I went with Herschell to the edge of the porch. I wanted to offer to walk part-way home with him.

Herschell said, "S'long."

I said, "See you."

My heart was beating hard. I was afraid Mother would come to the door. I was afraid she would say, "Arch Baxter, you'll catch your death. What on earth? What on earth are you thinking about?"

I was thinking that maybe Herschell would turn around and call to me. I was thinking maybe he would say, "What about some carom tomorrow?"

I hurried inside. Mother was in the kitchen. I started upstairs.

"Arch? Is that you?"

"It's me. It's I. I." I began coughing.

"Gargle. And take two aspirin. It's time for aspirin. Can you hear me, Arch? Are you hearing me?"

Herschell had left the stove lighted. After I had gargled and taken two aspirin, I sat close against the fire, wishing I were named Herschell Barnes, saying my own name. Miss Grange was always saying, "A man will lay down his life for his friend." I would have laid down my life for Herschell.

Archer Lee Baxter is a slow man.

Iᴛ must have been six months before I pieced Mother's hints and innuendoes together with what Ed Hoskin told me one afternoon while we were trading stamps.

Mr. Barnes wasn't the real father of any of his children. When he was drunk he would go into Webster's barber shop or the pool hall and cry about the situation. Ed said Dr. Frank Martin was Herschell's father. Hadn't I noticed how much Herschell looked like Dr. Martin? "Everybody knows. It beats all, doesn't it?"

I confronted Mother with the story. She shook her head sadly. "I didn't want you to know, Arch. I wanted to protect you."

That was a dark day. The story of the Barneses was as devastating to me as newspaper stories about plane wrecks and hurricanes.

Had I turned into a novelist I would probably have written about Mr. Barnes, who was handy with his hands, who drank, who sometimes ushered at the First Presbyterian Church, who lived with four handsome children in a shotgun house down by the L and N station, who was married to a small woman with bright hair. I cannot remember the woman's face, or her first name, or the clothes she wore.

Ed Hoskin who, in the eighth grade, had a large collection of dirty comics, became lieutenant governor under a Republican administration.

Herschell quit school in the eleventh grade to marry Tooli Cooper. He was killed by the midnight train at Dead Man's curve, leaving Tooli and three small children. Mother said it was a great tragedy.

Amaryllis & the Telephone

THE AMARYLLIS was about to come out. The time was dusk, a kind of green dusk. It was Tuesday. Mary Thomas stood in the hall by the table that held the telephone and the amaryllis. Walter had already finished eating. She had given him a nice supper—chicken salad, new peas, iced tea. Walter said, "You cook better than anybody."

"Silly. You're just hungry. And I have rolls. The rolls are hot and ready." Walter would eat anything. He would eat poison if you fixed it up for him with butter and mayonnaise.

"Sit down," Walter said. "Aren't you going to eat?" He slashed butter on one roll, two, three rolls, even though they were already buttered.

"I've already eaten." It wasn't a lie exactly. She had tasted some of the chicken salad while she was putting it together.

The dishwasher finished with the dishes. The house was quiet.

She locked the back door and the front door and the door to the basement. She had already drawn all the venetian blinds and the drapes, even in Mother Thomas' room.

Walter read the New York *Times* in the living room. Walter took to retirement like a duck to water; even when he worked he was semi-retired. Every day he came home from the insurance office to take a nap. Now he could spend all day with his books about the Civil War, taking naps and reading the New York *Times*. Walter was on the South's side. The *Times* took two days to come to Athens, Ohio, by mail. The world could end on Sunday and they wouldn't know it until Tuesday. Walter was satisfied. He took his pills from Dr. Gratz—high blood pressure, hiatal hernia, stomach—the Lord Himself couldn't know what all the pills were for. But Walter was happy; he liked to take pills; he was as contented as a baby on a schedule; Walter was such a baby himself he didn't mind not having children.

She was always busy. She barely had time to make a telephone call to anybody, even the people they used to go out with—to a movie, or a picnic at Dow Lake, or a lecture at the university—before Mother Thomas came to live with them permanently. A house took a lot of care. She was a fine house-keeper, if she did say so herself. Keeping the plants healthy was a full-time job. The window end of the living room looked like the Cincinnati Conser-vatory, absolutely gorgeous. She didn't talk to the plants, that was a silly idea; but the plants liked her. You could tell they liked her. Maybe Baby Amaryllis wanted to live in the window at the end of the living room. But she didn't complain. Her leaves almost sounded as they unfolded, like the clicks of a telephone dial.

It was nice to have a house with a little center hall. You could stand in the center hall and look into the living room and your own bedroom at the same time. It was a marvelously convenient house. Mary Thomas had been a smart woman. She had had the house built to her very own specifications. You had to take only a few steps from the hall to look into any room in the house.

Mother Thomas' room looked like anybody's spare bedroom now. You'd never dream the old lady had yelled her lungs out lying on that bed, tearing at the sheet. She had been strong as a horse, clear to the end. Mother Thomas had been strong enough to tear sheets.

Mary Thomas tiptoed back to the center hall.

She wished she was named Amaryllis. Amaryllis Belfontaine, or some-thing like that, like a character on a television program. A person could have her name changed. Actors were always having their names changed. You could go down to the courthouse and sign something, a paper of some kind.

"This is Amaryllis calling," a person could say to the telephone. A person could dial some of the letters in AMARYLLIS, long distance. It would be inter-esting to see who answered. She thought about saying, "Quietly, Baby," to the amaryllis.

She was happy. She was feeling good now. After Mother Thomas' passing she had been sickly, not bad sick, just not up to snuff. Everything was just fine now. Mother Thomas had left them all the money. Walter's sister could be as furious as she wanted to be. Walter's sister never had loved her mother. Walter's sister resented every day of Mother Thomas' life.

They hadn't seen the Pipkins forever, six months, eight, not since the funeral. They hadn't seen anybody. The Pipkins sent a lovely basket of carnations and delphinium. The Pipkins appreciated Walter's taking care of their insurance program. Walter was touched with the basket, as touched as Walter was likely to get.

"We need to get out, Walter. We need to see people." She sat gracefully on Walter's ottoman. She could see into the center hall. The night-light that glowed forever showed the amaryllis and the telephone.

He looked over his glasses at her. He began fiddling with that one strand of hair. He would look better if he shaved his head.

"You're looking at me. I'm people." Walter had a fairly nice sense of humor.

"I know, Silly." Amaryllis Thomas was a much prettier name than Lillian Pipkin. "The Pipkins, for instance. I don't know when we've seen hide or hair of them."

"Sure." Walter did not lower his eyes, but you could tell he wanted to. "I'm reading a review about a new book about the War Between the States. I can't wait to see which side wins."

To be reading about the Civil War in the New York *Times* was certainly a big thrill for Walter. For years he had been making jokes about wanting to see which side won. She laughed anyhow. It was a pretty good joke. Walter had been born in Millersburg, Kentucky. He liked to act as if Millersburg was as big as Philadelphia.

"But we need to get out. To mix."

"Invite somebody. We're feeling good now, aren't we? We're well." He would have said, "Invite somebody," even if she hadn't been forcing him to say the words. They had a good life together. They were good enough for each other. It was good to know you had a good life with somebody.

She said, "What about the Lewises?"

"Lewises who?"

"The Stones?"

"Stones who?"

"Shirley and Andy, Silly. The people with all those children. At church. Back when we used to go to church. Before Mother Thomas moved in with us permanently."

It was easy to mention Mother Thomas to Walter now. It was as easy as talking about philodendron.

And they were lucky not to have children, finally lucky. It was Walter's fault. Dr. Gratz said so, right out, before both of them.

It had been Walter's idea to stop going to church, months before Mother Thomas got really sick, a year, maybe two years. Mary Thomas had protested a little, but not much. Church always made her sleepy. And she couldn't carry a tune in a bucket. Walter had kept going to church with his mother and his wife because he liked to sing bass. He sang louder than anybody. It was embarrassing to sit beside him. After she gave him the *Hymns, Hymns, Hymns* album, he didn't need to go to church anymore. He sang along with the album. He had a nice voice, deep; when you held a hymnal with him you could feel his voice in the binding. That was a long time ago.

"The Adamses?" she said.

"Adamses, who?" He was reading again.

"The Greans?"

"Greans?"

"Pipkins?"

"Why not?" Walter did not lift his eyes. It was the Sunday newspaper. This was Tuesday. The world hadn't ended yet, for all anybody knew.

"That was a nice party we went to at their place, out in the country, out there, a long time ago, when Mother Thomas first got sick. We had a baby-sitter for her. You remember, don't you?" She spoke slowly, as if she were a flower opening. "A lot of people. A whole lot of people."

Walter nodded. He would have nodded no matter what she said—if she had said, "I could be in love with Paul Pipkin. I could have an affair with him. He thinks I'm attractive. He said so. I had on that blue eyelet. He's young, even younger than I am."

She wasn't laughing, but she covered her mouth as if she were laughing at a funeral, in church, or somewhere.

Paul was a nice man. She would never dream of having an affair with any-body, not the way people had affairs on television in the afternoon. But Paul was nice. He was tall and handsome and thin, like a hero on the programs. His stomach didn't hang out over his belt. And he had a marvelous head of hair, black and stiff.

"It was a barbecue, don't you remember? Maybe Labor Day. They had a sheep, a whole sheep. And a pit, a real barbecue pit?"

13

Walter nodded. "Sure. The Pipkins are good friends."

"And they sent flowers, when Mother Thomas passed. Lillian called me after the funeral. Maybe she called a couple of times. And I think we had a note from Paul, in his own handwriting."

"Who else's handwriting would he write in?"

"Oh, Walter. You do have a terrible sense of humor."

Mother Thomas had had terrible health problems, one thing after another. Her daughter-in-law had been marvelous to her. Mother Thomas had been fed well, and kept clean. Mary Thomas gave the old woman her medicines regularly, up to the last. It was wrong to keep people alive after they should have been dead for a month, even a month.

The week before Mother Thomas died Walter stood in the doorway of his very own mother's room and said, "Hello, how're you feeling today, Mother?"

That last day when Mother Thomas was yelling and tearing at the sheet, he just said, "Hello, how're you feeling today, Mother?"

The heart pills looked like any other pills. All of the pills looked a lot alike. The special pills rested in the alabaster box that Mother Thomas was terribly proud of; the box had come from Florence, Italy, from a missionary, a long time ago, when Mother Thomas was a girl, if anybody could imagine Mother Thomas ever having been a girl.

"Careful of the pills; they're powerful," old Dr. Gratz said over and over. Old Dr. Gratz said everything over and over. Dr. Gratz said, "Guard the pills, Mary. Guard the pills."

She moved from Walter's ottoman to her big chair and ottoman on the other side of the coffee table. "Anything good on television? Sometimes I forget what's on Tuesday night. Tuesday night is a hard night to remember."

Walter shook his head without looking at her. He turned another page of the paper. Walter was prissy, folding the paper carefully, making sure all the edges fit.

She read the Athens *Messenger*, Tuesday's *Messenger*, all the way through. She knew about things Walter didn't know. She read "Dear Abby" twice; she read the funnies twice; she read the death notices, even about people from Albany, and Coolville, and Pomeroy.

After all this time she still remembered the Pipkins' telephone number.

But she looked it up anyway. She was right. She had a good memory. Walter was always forgetting things. He'd forgot her birthday last month. He didn't even remember the anniversary of his mother's death, the tenth of January. Mary Thomas remembered the tenth of every month as regularly as the calendar leaves changed. Walter would forget his head if it wasn't screwed on his shoulders. He probably didn't remember the Pipkins' barbecue at all.

The amaryllis watched her fingers add up the numbers. Five and zero and two and four and one and five and six made twenty-three. She was very good at numbers. Walter practically counted on his fingers. It was a wonder he had ever been able to make a living at insurance. He had old Miss McPherson, of course. Old Miss McPherson had been good at numbers. Muriel McPherson had been dead longer than Mother Thomas. Old Muriel died of some kind of food poisoning. She was a glutton. She was like Walter that way—she would eat anything.

"Hello. Hello."

It wasn't Paul's voice.

"Hello. I must have the wrong number. I was calling the Pipkins, the Paul Pipkins."

"I'm Paul. How are you?"

"Amaryllis. Amaryllis. But you aren't Paul. I know you aren't. I know Paul Pipkin's voice."

"My name is Paul Pipkin." He sounded like somebody on television, in the program where people pretended to be somebody else. The voice was funny.

"You aren't Paul." She imagined the real Paul and his nice smile wrinkling the corners of his eyes. "But all right. Oh, all right. Is Lillian there? May I speak to Lillian, please?"

"Right here. She's in the family room. She's right here in the family room."

The petals of the amaryllis sounded like breathing, breaths, little short breaths.

Mary Thomas thought about calling Walter. Her voice could turn away from the telephone receiver and say, "Walter. Come help me, Walter."

"Hel-lo."

It wasn't Lillian's voice. Mary Thomas had a good ear for voices, even if she couldn't carry a tune.

It was a man's voice, talking in falsetto. Maybe the man was squeezing his nose; on one of those programs sometimes husbands even fooled their wives, when the wives were blindfolded.

"Lillian here," the man said again. "How are you sailing, Amaryllis? How would you like for me, just one girl to another . . ."

She knew what the man was going to say. She didn't allow herself to hear what he was saying.

She pretended she hadn't heard what he was saying. That was the way you were supposed to react to obscene phone-callers. "Lillian Pipkin. I'm calling for Lillian. I want them to come for dinner. Sunday. Sunday night. This is Tuesday. At seven. When it's dusk, green dusky time." She laughed naturally.

"My name is Lillian Pipkin." The man was laughing, but his laugh was like fingernails scratched across a blackboard. Once, a long time ago, she had hung up a little blackboard over the sink, to write down the things she wanted to buy at the A and P. "Potatoes, almond paste, V8." Sometimes Walter would come into the kitchen when she didn't know he was home. Sometimes he scratched his fingernails on the blackboard. He almost scared her to death. She didn't know why she had left the blackboard up for so long, for years and years, until Mother Thomas left Walter's sister to come live with them, forever and forever.

"We wanted the Pipkins to come to dinner. We wanted Lillian and Paul Pipkin to come to our house for dinner. We haven't seen them forever. We haven't seen anybody, not forever, not really since Mother Thomas passed away. It was heart. It was heart, finally. The flowers you sent were perfectly beautiful."

Lillian was talking vulgarly. You couldn't believe what Lillian was saying.

"We wanted to see you, Lillian. We both want to see you. We need to see people. We need to touch people."

The blossoms exhaled, three of them, four, perhaps there were four.

"Lillian, no. Don't talk that way. No please. We've been such very good friends, best friends, really. That barbecue. Walter and I were just talking about the barbecue, a whole sheep slaughtered; it was a marvelous party, Lillian." She was not crying, but she thought about crying. Mother Thomas had a clean mouth. Whatever else you said about Mother Thomas, she had a clean mouth. In front of Mother Thomas you were ashamed to say "darn it."

"Create in us clean hearts," Mother Thomas used to say for luncheon groups.

"Bless the food we are about to receive," Walter always said, his eyes open, reaching for his fork before he said "Amen."

"Well, if you don't want to talk to me, go fuck yourself. To God damn fuckin' hell with you, whoever you are. Nobody's named Amaryllis."

"It's the name of a shepherdess." Mary Thomas kept her voice low. "I learned about it in high school. She's used in poetry. I used to read a lot of poetry, even after Mother Thomas moved in with us. I used to write poetry, too, when it rained, or when I was lonely, or," she was whispering, "when I had my periods."

"Nobody's named Amaryllis. Shit."

"Call me back. Please call me back. I'm Mary Thomas." She began to spell her name, but the telephone had already clicked. She pressed it hard against her ear; there was no sound; if there was any sound it was only a faint scratching noise.

"I am Mary Amaryllis Thomas. Good-bye Amaryllis." The telephone was as quiet as the pot which held the lovely blossoms. Flowers did not, do not, sound. Even if they did, do, the sound was, is, only a gentle humming, like music from another room.

Walter had turned on the television. He was watching an old movie. He had not been listening to her. She almost wished Walter had been listening.

Walter lay on the little couch that divided the dining area from the living room. The couch wasn't long enough for a dog. Walter was over five feet eight. She wished he wasn't allergic to dogs. All these years it would have been very nice to have had a dog. You could name a dog anything you wanted to, even a flower's name. You could call a dog anything you wanted to, male or female. Walter had his head on one armrest. His feet hung over the other armrest; it was amazing what contortions Walter could get himself into, like a lady in a circus. Walter's mother loved to go to circuses.

On the huge screen Alice Faye was singing. Walter said, "She was a great actress. She has a fine voice."

"Great. Fine." She sat in her chair beside the coffee table and put her feet on her ottoman.

She waited a long time, but the telephone did not ring.

She thought about telling Walter about the man who pretended to be Paul and pretended to be Lillian. From where she sat she could see not only the big television screen—the biggest screen Walter could buy—but also the center hall and the table which held the amaryllis and the telephone. The table had belonged to her great grandmother. Back then nobody would have wondered about what a telephone meant. A telephone meant calling somebody. It meant, "Come to dinner." We are real people who pass dishes to each other: meat, sliced roast, and creamed potatoes, with cheese, and salad, Jello with bing cherries, and little dishes, pickled onions and celery hearts, and, for dessert, meringues, with strawberries whether or not they were in season. A long time ago she had served dinners to people. She was a marvelous cook, if she did say so herself. But somehow she didn't get hungry much anymore.

Walter slept, snored, waking himself up to sleep and snore and wake again.

She waited.

Alice Faye was in an automobile accident. She was getting well. The man, whatever his name, Walter Something? Paul Something? stood beside her bed. Mary Thomas slowly removed her feet—she was wearing house slippers that looked like ballet slippers—from her ottoman; she rose gracefully from her chair. She was as graceful as Alice Faye. And she was thinner. Alice Faye had been what you would call fat.

Walter said, "Wait. It's almost over. They're going to get back together, the woman and the man." Walter didn't know Alice Faye's name from his own mother's.

"I'm going to call the Pipkins to come to dinner on Saturday, Sunday, I mean. You said it was all right."

Walter was watching Alice Faye get out of bed. The man was holding her up. The man put his arm under her armpit; actually, he was touching her right breast.

"Sure," Walter said. He would have said "Sure" if she had said, "Walter, I am going to kill you. I'm going to kill myself." She could have said, "We have enough pills, Walter."

She said, "The Pipkins. Sunday night, at seven, at dusk."

"Sure."

She checked the number with the telephone book. She checked the number with her address book. Both numbers added up to twenty-three.

It was Paul's voice.

"Paul. It's Mary, Mary Thomas. I've been trying to call you. Have you been out, Paul? Have you answered?"

"Nobody's called. It's good to hear you, Mary. We've been here all evening. We're watching television. An old movie. You want to talk to Lillian? How's Walter? Is Walter fine?" Paul was mannerly. He couldn't really be interested in Walter's health.

"He's watching television, too. Walter's watching a news analysis, on Educational T.V. Walter's crazy about the news. He knows everything the New York *Times* knows—two days ago."

Paul was laughing with her. Paul had a nice laugh. "Here's Lillian. We were just talking about you two, not long ago."

"We've been talking about you, too. We've been missing you. Lillian? Oh, it's you, Lillian. I've been calling and calling. I got somebody funny, funny people. I was afraid it was you. I was afraid somebody was holding a gun on you. I don't like to think about you way out in the country, without any neighbors."

"Really, Mary. We have neighbors. It's nice to hear you. We're fine. We love it out here. Except we miss seeing friends."

"Please. Yes. No. We wanted you to come for supper Sunday. For dinner, at night."

"Let me check. I'm sure we can. I hope we can."

It was easy to imagine Lillian, looking young, probably wearing something pink, as pink as amaryllis blossoms, light pink, a hostess gown, like Alice Faye's a long time ago. "We aren't doing anything Sunday night, are we, Paul?" Lillian Pipkin was calling to Paul Pipkin in a night house in the country. Lillian and Paul Pipkin had stopped watching television to talk about next Sunday night, their windows opened to the fields where shepherds and shepherdesses with strange names watched fog cover the backs of their adorable sheep, before they made love, Paul and Lillian. "We'd love to," Lillian said.

"If we don't answer, keep knocking. We'll probably be out back. Walter loves to barbecue. We have a new barbecue grill." She imagined a barbecue grill, shining scarlet and silver, big enough for a slaughtered sheep.

"It's so nice of you to call. We'll look forward to Sunday. We don't get out enough. We're all too young to be stick-in-the muds, stuck-in-the-muds."

"Oh yes, Lillian. You have such a nice way of expressing yourself." They were laughing together. Lillian had a marvelous sense of humor. "Until Sunday."

"What's that? What's that?" The movie was over. Suddenly Walter was as inquisitive as a billy goat.

"They're coming, the Pipkins. It's time to go to bed, Walter. It's time, right now."

The amaryllis flowers, four, five, sounded as angry as a telephone in an empty house ringing late at night.

A Hundred Paths

WE WERE OLD, not old, but not young. There were the four of us, my wife's college roommate, her husband, my wife, and I. We had known each other for almost thirty years. "My God," we said, laughing as if what we said were not true; "Not that long!" imagining somebody else's saying, "Not that long!" wanting to believe somebody else.

We had met when we were eighteen in a registration line at the University of Kentucky.

And then it is Labor Day, thirty years later, and Susan and I are visiting the Robinsons again. We were on our way home to Ohio from the Cape. Susan called Peg from Chatham. "Of course you'll stop for a visit, for a month or two," Peg shouted. Susan, smiling in the telephone booth, held the receiver toward me. Susan laughed loudly in the booth. "Two nights," she said. "I won't even check with Leonard." She raised her eyebrows, checking with me. I nodded. I felt good. There was sun, and the sound of traffic could have been the ocean. Susan said, "You'll have a marvelous dinner ready for us tonight, around seven?" Peg said, "Absolutely marvelous. You've never eaten such food. And tomorrow a picnic at the park."

They were yelling at each other, as if they were eighteen in a registration line at the University of Kentucky.

For years we have visited each other on our ways to other places. Both the Robinsons and we have moved three times in twenty-odd years; from small towns, to cities, to the far edges of cities; from impossible little apartments, to suburbs where everybody's roses matched his neighbors', to rather handsome houses with high ceilings and long lawns. Now the Robinsons boast a tidy red barn at their Rochester place.

The Robinsons have a daughter, Jennifer. We are the parents of young Leonard. We grew up in a pre-pill period, but we were careful.

"We're parallel lines," Peg said after the marvelous dinner, as she has said for thirty years. We had eaten and drunk too much. We sat opposite each other, on the love seats Peg bought in Indianapolis twenty years ago.

"And we always say *we*, don't we?" Susan said, as I knew she was going to say. They could have been comparing lives over Coca-Colas at Dunn's Drug Store almost a third of a century ago.

Peg said, "Other people say, *I*. Cheryl Roethke—she's the woman down the road—you met her last time—Cheryl says *my* bedroom, and they sleep together. Harry's closet is in *her* bedroom."

Clarke said, "Come on, Peggy. You're not making sense." Clarke is a tall, thin, handsome man. I am always surprised at his handsomeness. I do not dwell on my height or my poundage.

"She's making absolute sense." Susan was sleepy. "Generally *two* people can't say *we*. We're *four* people, and we say *we*!"

"We, we, we," Clarke said. "We ought to go to bed. We've got to be alert for Peggy's fine picnic at the park."

"It's going to be a perfectly fantastic picnic—we don't know how to have any other kind. Do you remember in Lexington when we . . ."

"And then we came back to our house and my aunts were there, all five of them, and we . . ."

"But you haven't told us nearly enough about Jennifer's job in New York, and . . ."

"And Leonardcito's really going to the Woodrow Wilson school? When I think about . . ."

"Whatever happened to that young man Jennifer was so crazy about, the one she met that summer in Vienna?"

"She's over that—him—a long time ago."

I suppose that through the years Clarke and I have been listeners. We are peripheral friends. We were not roommates. For a while Clarke "dated" Susan quite seriously. I "dated" Peg. The word "dated" sounds a very long time ago.

"There's somebody else now, named Paulsie, if you can imagine." Peg ran her tongue over her lips. "Honestly, sometimes I wonder . . ."

Mostly the girls talked about when Jennifer and the other Leonard were young.

Clarke said, "We're not old enough to spend an evening talking about our children."

But we talked about our children.

Susan said, "They're good kids. They've turned out well."

"We have so much to be thankful for. Finally—maybe finally." Peg had tears in her eyes.

"But we mustn't say that." Susan was crying. She leaned forward, her hands over her head, her fingers crossed.

"We *can* say," Peg said. "We can say it so far. They aren't in jail, and they aren't maniacs, and . . ."

Susan said, "Not so far as we know. But we don't know very far."

Peg said, "You make me sick, Susan. You're always negative. Forever you've been negative."

"Well, I beg your most humble pardon."

Clarke said, "Hear, hear."

It was not a quarrel. I cannot remember a real quarrel with the Robinsons.

Peg said, "I know what you mean. You know I know what you mean."

"I know, I know," Susan and Peg said together.

We had another drink before we went to bed.

I dreamed of all of us when we were young. I do not remember seeing our present faces or bodies in the dream. Five or six times I woke in the night, but it was a continued dream. I make nothing of it. I haven't been sleeping well these last few months, this last year, since I became chairman of the board of Amalgamated Enterprises, Susan's father's Enterprises. Once we were poor. Once I taught English in a high school.

In the dream Peg said, "We are well to do." In the dream I did not know what the words meant. I said, in the dream, "What does *well to do* mean, Peg Robinson?" Susan said, "Everyone knows what well to do means, Leonard Wayne!"

Twice in the night Susan woke me. "You're all right, honey. You're just having a bad dream."

We were late getting off to the picnic. Clarke and I walked their three dogs to the village, bought a couple of papers. The day was hot; the day pretended it would never be autumn, but leaves fell from the ginkgo trees in the Robinsons' yard. Clarke said, "They look like butterflies, or warblers, falling."

I said, "Sure enough. You're a major poet." Clarke was in public relations before he became a university vice-president in charge of regional branches.

Clarke laughed genuinely. "The University of Kentucky was a long time ago, wasn't it?"

We ate a slow breakfast. Peg said, "You weren't annoyed with me last night, Leonard? You don't think I'm a foolish woman, almost fifty years old? Susan wasn't annoyed last night. She promised me she wasn't annoyed. And she's not negative. She's the most positive thinker I have ever had the pleasure of meeting."

We laughed together.

THE park belongs to Clarke's university. There is a lake, and a little theater, and paths, a hundred paths. Some alumnus willed a hundred paths to the university. Lately I am interested in the nature of wills, and human vanity. My estate, our estate, goes, of course, to Susan and Leonard. But I am pleased with the thought of a man who has written on a legal document: "One hundred paths." I would like for Susan and Leonard to remember me as capable of such a will.

The parking lot was full of small orange and yellow and red cars.

"Park there," Peg said. "There's a place. We look like a hearse, don't we? A hearse among the butterflies?" The Robinsons have always driven large dark cars.

We laughed.

Susan said, "I'm always proud to ride in your cars. Our next car will be large and dark."

"Careful, Susan. You mustn't ruffle me." Peg was laughing louder than any of us.

"Yes, yes, Little Horse." It was a joke from thirty years ago whose significance I do not remember.

Clarke seemed to remember. Peg was convulsed. When she caught her breath she said, "If there are a lot of people at the picnic tables, I don't think I want to go. We'll go back home and eat. I think I don't want to be here."

Clarke said, "Don't be a goose." Susan said, "Really, Peg!"

There were dozens of places for us above the lake. A whole slope of tables waited under fine old maple and oak trees. Evidently the butterfly cars had brought only swimmers. Clarke, the vice-president, explained, "After all,

24

school's out. School hasn't started yet. These are the workers and the dregs. These are only the dregs. It's Labor Day."

Peg chose a middle table. "Marvelous. This is absolutely marvelous. Look, these grills, they're new, Clarke. And the tables are new. Look, just look."

"Absolutely. Marvelous," Susan said.

The girls' voices were young. I looked from Susan to Peg. Clarke was looking, too.

"We will take a walk." Peg plopped her fat handbag onto the table. "A man's place is at the grill; woman's place is taking a walk."

Clarke said, "Come off it, Peggy."

I was disappointed, too. I have inherited my friends from Susan. Perhaps, once, Susan and Clarke slept together. Our generation has not talked openly about such matters. I said, "Beware of rapists."

Clarke said, "And bears. There are bears in those woods."

Peg said, "We can handle them. We're liberated."

Susan placed her fat purse beside Peg's. She was giggling. I am grateful that Susan can still giggle. "You'll guard our luggage."

Peg tripped as she started up the slope. The girls laughed as if nothing in the wide world could have been funnier.

It was ridiculous to have worried over being left alone with Clarke. I genuinely enjoy Clarke. He talked about his work, the drop in enrollment, budget problems, his president's "thrusts." I traded business talk, about the energy crisis and strip mining.

Clarke started the fire. Slowly the charcoal briquettes oozed into flame.

For spaces of time we were quiet, looking down at the lake where very young men and women dived and shouted and pushed each other from platforms and floating logs.

Below us appeared a figure wearing a T shirt and blue and white striped shorts, waving to somebody in the water. The figure was thin, its hair wet, curling at its shoulders.

Idly I said, "Boy or girl? Young Leonard's hair is that long, even longer." I have tried not to worry over Leonard. I have pretended not to worry.

"Boy, I guess."

"I guess so."

25

The figure turned, moved toward one of the hundred paths. I nodded to her, feeling invisible.

"Hi," she said. She walked beautifully. "Oh, hello, Mr. Robinson. Hello." She smoothed her hands over her hair.

"Hello there. This is my friend, Leonard Wayne, a long-time friend."

"How do you do?" we asked each other. We assured each other that it was a lovely day.

When she disappeared down the path, I said, "She's very much a girl. I'm sorry. It's hard to tell about sex any more."

"What are you sorry for? She works in the Treasurer's Office. That's why she's here during vacation. I can't remember her name."

"She's pretty." I felt close to Clarke Robinson. I felt that he was my friend.

"Sure." Clarke was looking into the trees where the girl had disappeared. Perhaps he had slept with her. "She's going to the meadow. Jennifer kept bees down there, when we first moved to Rochester. We had great honey for a couple of years. It was a Girl Scout project, 4-H, something."

"I probably wouldn't know Jennifer."

"That girl, that other girl, not Jennifer, she's probably meeting somebody. They'll probably make love, have sex, whatever you want to call it. In the bushes, or a car, maybe back in her room on campus. We have mixed dormitories, very mixed."

I said, "They've come a long way. We've come a long way." I wondered if Susan and Clarke had slept together.

"Sure." Clarke's eyes looked hard at me.

I said, "But we're lucky. Peg and Susan are right. We're lucky with our kids. Susan worries too much. She thinks Leonard is sleeping with somebody, a Chinese girl. I suppose he is."

Always before we had been people in a registration line, friends of a family, waiting in a queue.

"Paulsie," Clarke said, "the Paulsie Peg mentioned last night. Jennifer called day before yesterday. That's why it's good you are here. Jennifer is madly in love with him. I assume it's a him. They're living together. I try not to assume anything these days." Clarke did not lower his eyes.

I said, "I'll say. Young people will be young people." It is a foolish sentence I have often said to Susan. Perhaps I have never been young.

A Hundred Paths

"Peg hasn't slept. Last night she kept saying, 'Should I tell them? Shouldn't I tell our best friends?' You're our best friends, Leonard. You're people we don't see much. What do you think of that, Leonard boy?"

I said, "Sure."

Clarke said, "I'm sorry we had children, a child."

I said, "A boy is easier, I guess. Less open. With me, at least. Susan has talked to him about the girl. Her name is Lois." For no reason that I can identify I wanted to exchange a confidence with this man who sat across from me at a picnic table in a park. I do not own many confidences. I have lived carefully, a good steward to the monies Susan has inherited. "Susan and Leonard had a terrible conversation. I listened from another room. I didn't join them. I was a coward."

Clarke looked down at his hands. His fingers were spread far apart. He said, "God damn you, Leonard. I wouldn't dream of talking to Jennifer." He seemed capable of crying. I felt as close to him as if we were strangers in a falling plane, determined to identify ourselves before we disappeared.

I said, "I hadn't any experience to speak of, when Susan and I were married. We were young."

Clarke closed his fingers. He wears a wedding ring. Susan did not give me a wedding ring. "I don't want Leonard to be branded," she said in Dunn's. Peg said, "Honestly, Susan, you are too dumb to listen to."

I have been faithful to Susan. I am a coward.

Clarke said, "I've tried to make up for it." I did not know exactly what he meant, but I heard the sound of the plane's falling. "It's, the whole business, I guess it's harder for women, wives, of our generation." Twice, according to Susan, Clarke and Peg were ready for a divorce. Clarke had a girl in Harrodsburg and another in Indianapolis.

I said, "Whatever that means." I was embarrassed. I am embarrassed to be forty-eight years old.

I did not mean to lower my eyes to look at my wristwatch. The girls had been gone for over half an hour.

"You're worried about them?"

"No. I guess so. Susan doesn't have any sense of time or direction. She gets lost easily."

Again Clarke spread his hands on the table. He pushed himself up. He stepped gracefully over the bench. "I'll go find them. Guard the fire. We could use a couple more briquettes."

We did not look at each other.

Clarke was gone for a long time.

I watched the young people in the water.

I picked up the fat purses and started up the slope.

I did not want to appear ridiculous, a man carrying two ladies' purses. I went back to the table.

I started the steaks. I was afraid I had started them too soon. I took them off the grill and put them back. I was lucky with the steaks. I was ready to take them off again when Clarke and the girls came scuffling down the hill. The girls were laughing so loudly that a man on a farther path stopped to look at them.

Clarke said, "I found them swinging on grapevines, with three bears and three rapists."

Peg said, "And we overcame them, every one."

Susan said, "You weren't worried, were you, Worry-Box?"

I said, "Chow. Chow's on." I beat on the grill. I do not like a man who says such things as "Chow's on."

I received compliments.

Peg said, "There have never been such perfectly cooked steaks, not in the history of the world."

Susan said, "Peg makes the kind of potato salad they serve in heaven."

Clarke was as jolly as the girls. He said, "Leonard, old man, you missed your calling." He spoke as if we had never talked almost honestly to each other.

We have had such picnics before. We said, we, we, we. We said, "Do you remember?"

It was Peg's idea to take a walk. "We exercise, or burst. The meadow. We haven't been to the meadow forever, not since that silly project of Jennifer's."

We said words like "Great" and "Fine" and "Sure."

I t was a long walk to the meadow. There was a kind of road at first, not big enough for a car, too wide for a path. We walked four together at first. There were little hills, up and down, and up again. Paths left the road, and returned. Some of the paths appeared to be shortcuts.

We walked in twos.

I walked by myself behind three people, behind two. My breath came hard. I tried to measure my breathing. We were all the same age. I was angry that my breathing was difficult.

The road was a cave of trees. The trees smelled like a cave. The cave was a tunnel. Relax, I told myself. I am enjoying the walk alone, behind three, two, one; I have no sense of urgency, alone.

Finally the three stood at the edge of the meadow.

Clarke turned to call to me. "I don't recognize anything."

The meadow was like a picture of a meadow. It had been recently mowed. The meadow was an oasis. It was a clean plate.

"They used this for a playing field, for a while," Clark said. "Maybe they still do."

Susan and Peg are good tourists. "Beautiful," they said. "Glorious."

The sky had clouded. The meadow held an underwater light.

"I'm remembering." Clarke was a tourist guide. "There's an abandoned railroad bridge over there in front of us, on the other side of the meadow." Clarke pointed. His forefinger seemed larger than his hand.

Beyond the far trees stood the lattice of a railroad bridge.

Susan said, "Too bad about railroads."

Peg said, "Do you remember when we took the children to Cincinnati, to the zoo, on the train?"

We remembered.

"Over there," Clarke said. "That's where Jennifer had her bees."

"It's marvelous," Peg said. "I can't wait to go home so we can come back again." Years ago Peg had first said the sentence, at Natural Bridge in Kentucky.

Clarke said, "It's a playing field all right. I can't keep up with everything that happens at the university."

Susan, standing in the center of the meadow, turned slowly. "I'm making a wish. But I mustn't tell the wish. When you make a wish in the center of a meadow, it always comes true." She smiled at Clarke as she turned.

I said, "Meadow or wish?" I wondered if all the paths led to the meadow. Peg started to turn, too. "I am wishing, I am wishing."

The girls moved beautifully, like figures in a ballet. Clarke was watching them.

An engine sounded on the other side of the meadow.

Slowly Susan and Peg stopped turning.

The angry sound of a motor moved from right to left, from maples to willows.

Clarke said, "That can't be a car. There's no road over there."

"It's a motorcycle," Peg said. "It's twenty motorcycles."

"No. There's not any road. You remember when Jennifer had the bees, and we walked over there."

The sound stopped, and started again, and stopped.

"It's a motorcycle," Susan said. "I'm glad young Leonard never wanted a motorcycle." Her voice was loud.

We stood listening. I thought of reaching out for the hands beside me. We could have been a row of paper soldiers, cut from folded newspapers. I wondered what Susan had wished, turning in the meadow. I had not thought of making a wish. I do not know what I would have wished for.

The meadow was as quiet as a bowl of water, left long standing.

The sound returned.

The four of us started toward the sound. Paper soldiers can run quickly. I was tired. I remembered the face of Jennifer and young Leonard in the dream. I did not want to think about the dream.

I ran ahead of the others. I stumbled out of the other side of the meadow, to an embankment, pulling myself up by branches, dogwood and sassafras. Leaves fell from my hands. A branch snapped Clarke in the face. "Sorry, old man." The girls moved from the meadow behind us, mounting the bank.

Boards lay across the railroad tracks. A dirt road, a real dirt road, led up to the bridge.

Clarke said, "My God."

Two people on a throbbing motorcycle waited in the very center of the bridge. They leaned far to the right, looking down into the river. The person in front, the larger one, revved the motor. The couple wore blue jeans and checked shirts with long sleeves. They were surely a boy and a girl. They roared across the bridge to somewhere.

Clarke said, "God damn." Susan and Peg stood with us at the side of the dirt road. The girls and Clarke breathed heavily. I was pleased that they were breathing heavily.

We waited.

Susan spoke quietly. "There's a woman's shift hanging on a dogwood tree down there. And a pair of shorts, cut-off blue jeans. Did you notice?"

"And a white dress draped over a sassafras bush. And two necklaces, something gold." Peg was whispering.

Susan said, "And a ring. I saw a ring on top of the shorts, a high school ring, maybe. Leonard had one. Do you remember?" She was smiling as if she had wished a good wish in the meadow and received an answer.

I did not remember. I had not noticed anything.

Peg said, "And once we came to the meadow and Jennifer . . ."

Clarke said, "God damn it, shut up."

I suppose the four of us heard the car at the same time. We listened together, looking at each other. I felt very close to Susan and the Robinsons. Because we listened together I felt we were wearing the same face.

A car appeared. It was a tan two-door Chevrolet, four or five years old. It stopped at the edge of the bridge, not six feet from us.

A boy, no older than Leonard, opened the car door. He wore chinos, low slung, almost to his pelvis. His shirt was pink and white spring blossoms, opened but stuck into his trousers. He wore a ring on a chain around his neck.

He had a fine body, like Leonard's. His hair was long and yellow, neatly combed. I studied the comb marks in his hair.

A radio played softly in his car, rock music with a heavy beat. People sang. They said the same words over and over, but I could not distinguish the words.

The boy turned the radio volume high. Peg put her hands over her ears. Within, above the music, the boy got out of the car and closed his door. He did not look at us. We might have been trees watching. He walked around the front of the car to the other side. He opened the door on the other side. I cannot remember for how long he held the door open, looking into the car. It was as if he were letting something out, or letting something in.

He closed the door. He circled the car, returning to the bridge. He walked very slowly, as if he were counting his steps. He did not walk on to the road-bed of the bridge. He stopped at the very edge. He slanted his body against the right-hand truss. The truss of the bridge was rusted. Susan whispered, "Careful." I have not asked her what she meant. Perhaps she was worried that the boy would fall into the water. Perhaps she was afraid the rust would stain the blossoms of his shirt.

He could have been a figurehead on a ship.

Clarke said, "Let's go." I am sure it was Clarke who spoke, but we did not go.

After a while, perhaps after only a little while, the boy pushed himself to a standing position. He lighted a cigarette. He stood watching the water move under the bridge. The cigarette hung from his lips. He held his arms straight beside him, his fists clenched.

That evening at the Robinsons the girls could not talk enough about the boy, stating the afternoon.

Susan said, "Pot. I know he was smoking pot, or something worse."

Peg said, "Hostile. A sense of evil."

Susan said, "Those hands, those fists. He was about to explode."

Peg said, "A sense of orgy. Charged. The whole scene was charged."

Susan said, "If we had met him on our beautiful walk, he would have killed us."

Peg said, "One of us. He would have killed at least one of us."

I expected Clarke to say, "Come off it, Peggy." Instead he rose from his chair, the Lazy-Boy they had bought in Harrodsburg. "Refills," he said. "Refills all around."

"Why not?" Susan and Peg said together, lifting their empty glasses as if to toast the world.

I suppose we were all looking at each other.

At the bridge we had looked at each other, not looking.

At the bridge Clarke said, "Let's get the hell out of here."

I know the boy was waiting for us to leave. I know we left because he was waiting for us to leave.

I was the last down the hill. I tried to look hard at the boy by the side of the bridge. But I did not stay to see what was going to happen.

I have never stayed to see what was going to happen.

But I felt close to the boy.

Rain spit at us across the meadow. Susan and Peg and Clarke ran, as well as forty-eight-year-old people can run. Susan was ahead, then Peg, then Clarke. Clarke stopped to grab the picnic basket from our table on the slope. The road back is always shorter than the road away.

"You're coming. You're all right?" Clarke called over his shoulder.

"Hurry, hurry," the girls, the women, called.

I held back, not, I think, because I was not in good shape. For a moment, for only a moment, I thought about returning to the boy on the bridge.

In the dark car the others were wringing wet, too. They were breathing heavily, too.

Susan said, "You're drowned. You're absolutely drowned."

Peg said, "Here's a towel. Dry off. You'll catch your death."

I assured them I was fine. I said, "It was a very exciting outing."

Susan said, "You're positive?"

I said, "Positive."

Peg said, "We'll look for the road then. Hurry, Clarke. We'll find the road that goes over the railroad bridge. It has two ends. Surely it has two ends."

I do not think that Clarke really tried to find the road. I was relieved that he did not find it. Perhaps the others were relieved, too.

The rain did not last long. We went to a "Museum of Machinery, 1820 Until Now." The sign was written in old English letters. I insisted on paying for all of us. The cost was three dollars each.

It is winter now. I do not know why I have written what I have written. I am not trying to force significance from a picnic, and a meadow, and a railroad bridge.

Fortunato & the Night Visitor

MR. FORTUNATO Alberto Lowe believed in three things: the business of being a food broker, wine for the stomach's sake, and the memory of his remarkable mother. The first made his addiction to the second and third possible; the second and third made the first thoroughly palatable. All day, even on his fortieth birthday, October twenty-eighth, he sat at his neat desk in his office on Water Street and talked over the telephone. He received orders from food merchants who wanted meat or sugar or canned tomatoes. He telephoned the sellers of meat, sugar, and canned tomatoes. Without once rising from his foam rubber cushion, he arranged, lucratively, for the union of wanter and haver. He didn't think of anything all day.

Mr. Lowe's father, who started the business and acquired the very best national accounts, used to speak of his brokerage as a gustatory matrimonial bureau. He liked to consider the romance of Central Kentucky's families sitting down to the food he had arranged by telephone. Fortunato Alberto's mind, on the other hand, worked as automatically as the dial system. He did not think at all, even on his birthday, until after he had locked the office door at 5:30, taken a cab to the Fayette Hotel, where he had lived since his mother's death, walked up the fourteen flights of stairs to his apartment—he needed the exercise—telephoned the bar for a bottle of champagne, and placed a pile of Spanish songs and dances on his stereo. Then, and only then, did Mr. Lowe begin his pleasant thoughts.

He did not listen to the records, but he always played them. The music store down the street had an order of five years' standing: "Anything Spanish." The bright folders appealed to Mr. Lowe as a nice tribute to the memory of his musical mother who had named him Fortunato in the first place. Everybody in Lexington thought she was the limit to give him such a name. Mr. Lowe was named Wallace Clay, and Mrs. Lowe's father was Edward Hunt.

But Mrs. Lowe said, "Everybody in Lexington is named the same thing. It's high time somebody started something new!"

"But where on earth did you get the name?"

"I made it up. It just came to me—I was born with a veil over my face, you know," Mrs. Lowe said.

"Mary, you're a sight," everybody in Lexington said.

"Fortunato Alberto is going to be different." Mrs. Lowe fluffed the chiffon flower on her bosom and smiled. She had collected chiffon flowers, the way her son collected Spanish music.

Fortunato smiled at his water tumbler of champagne, remembering his mother's voice. He did not mind being forty in the least, and he could just hear everybody in Lexington say, "Mary, you're a sight." Sitting on his couch, facing the black marble mantel, drinking the wine and not listening to the music, he could think about the past of his mother as easily as he could think about his own past.

"It would have been better if I had been born with a veil over my face," Fortunato said to the tumbler, but not aloud.

"But I wasn't, I guess. And that's that."

Fortunato Alberto did not regret the factual. Although his mother had kept announcing for thirty-five years that her son was going to be different, he wasn't different—not excessively. He belonged to things, like Rotary; and he attended things, like the community concert series; and he gave two large dinners every year down in the Fayette Room. He was just like everybody else, only not so much. It was a conclusion he had come to on a number of evenings, and the conclusion bothered him no more on his fortieth birthday than on any other day. Perhaps it would have been better if he were not a philosopher, but he was a philosopher, and that, too, was that. Fortunato Lowe had majored in philosophy at Centre College, Danville, Kentucky.

Mrs. Lowe had wanted to send him some place like Montana State or a nice school in Alaska. Her husband said it was enough for the boy to be named what he was. Wallace C. rarely brought himself to speak his son's name, but he admired Mary Lowe as tremendously as everybody else did. They had a very satisfactory marriage. Mrs. Lowe gave in to Centre with practically no fuss. "Very well, Wallace C., you win," she said, reaching for her accordion. Mary Lowe played the accordion better than anybody in Lexington. "We're almost like everybody else in town, and I might as well accept it," she said. Mr. Lowe, pressing his victory, said, "We're exactly like everybody else in town. Montana State, indeed!"

Mrs. Lowe began to play her own intricate arrangement of "La Paloma." She laughed as merrily as if her husband had told one of his many funny jokes, proving that they had a good marriage. "But everybody else wasn't born with my veil," she said. She had him there, of course.

Mrs. Lowe was never a bore with her occult wisdom or second sight or mysticism or tomfoolery—whatever you want to call it. Mr. Lowe called it tomfoolery. Fortunato, a philosopher, didn't call it anything, but he liked to think about it. He liked to remember his mother's voice when he called long distance from Danville. "Hello, Fortunato Alberto," she would say before the operator had time to speak. "I know it's you, Fortunato Alberto." She was really uncanny. And over half the time she anticipated what the mailman was going to bring, and she was always dreaming about the cousins in Old Virginia the night before they died. It was all very interesting to think about, even if you didn't believe in it.

"I could conjure the devil if I wanted to," Mrs. Lowe often said. She laughed and plucked at her chiffon flower. "But I wear my veil casually."

"Mary, you're the limit," everybody in Lexington said.

When Fortunato was a little boy he had thought it would be very exciting to conjure the devil or his grandmother or Henry Clay or somebody—he was not particular. He used his chemistry set trying to conjure. When his parents found out, Mrs. Lowe reprimanded him; she threatened to make the set disappear. Mr. Lowe thought the whole business was a great joke. "It's nothing to laugh about," Mrs. Lowe said.

"You could handle the spirits for him all right," Mr. Lowe said. He was red in the face. He always got red in the face when he laughed at his own jokes. "You would handle them the way you handled Cousin Martha Smith."

"Wallace C., really," Mary Lowe said, smiling in spite of herself. Cousin Martha Smith was a family joke, even though the Lowes inherited her lovely home on Main Street and lived in it for twenty years. Cousin Martha was recovering from a heart attack when Mrs. Lowe paid her a sick call and allowed a sparrow to fly through the window. "You simply must have some good fresh air," Mrs. Lowe said, raising the window, and there was the sparrow fluttering against the pongee curtains. Cousin Martha's little bead eyes darted from the bird to Mrs. Lowe. "You, Mary. You and your witchcraft," Cousin Martha shouted, and promptly had another heart attack. Mr. Lowe considered it a great joke even at the time. But Mrs. Lowe wasn't able to laugh about it until Martha was up and out again.

"The Devil," Fortunato said aloud in his own hotel apartment, remembering the chemistry set box—blue and red with the word *chemistry* in gold letters as decorated with curlicues as the fireplace of Cousin Martha's bedroom. He almost never spoke aloud in his apartment, but he was not embarrassed at the sound of his own voice saying, "the Devil." After all it was his birthday, he told himself, emptying the glass.

Fortunato thought about his mother's chiffon flowers, but he promised her not to think about them as he poured his second glass—this time only a few fingers' worth. He did not feel the effects of the champagne, of course, but he felt very good. He could not remember a more pleasant evening of thinking. He was forty years old and he felt as good as that time when the professor read his paper on Hume aloud to the class. "I do not agree with the conclusions of this paper," the old man said, coughing into his fist. "We have here an admirable piece of work, however." He coughed again. "You have a very interesting mind, Mr. Lowe."

Fortunato telephoned his mother to tell her about the compliment. She told everybody in Lexington, of course. She telephoned Fortunato back the next day to tell him he must never stop thinking, not for a single minute. "You can live all your life in Central Kentucky without thinking," she said. "But you're different, Fortunato Alberto. I want you to be different." Her voice was clear and ringing over the wire, as melodious as an accordion.

Fortunato smiled at his own face in the black marble mantel. Perhaps he really resembled his mother. He frowned. He did not resemble her so much when he frowned. He smiled again. Many of the ladies who attended the Woman's Club at the hotel on Saturday afternoon commented on how much he favored Mary. Naturally Fortunato tried not to be in the lobby when the women congregated, but sometimes he was caught, and always somebody said that Mary Lowe would never be dead as long as he was alive.

It was difficult to frown, for he was approaching the most interesting part of his thinking.

He could not be positive, not Hume-positive, that it was his own round face which looked back at him from the slick surface of the mantel. He could not actually prove he was he, sitting on the couch, though he assumed he sat on the couch by the stereo and drank the wine at least five evenings out of the week. Perhaps, perhaps a philosopher would insist that it was his mother's round face smiling in the black mantel.

Fortunato Lowe did not believe in the spirit world. Yet he possessed—he truly possessed—proof of the spirit world through his remarkable mother, born with a veil over her face.

"The Devil," Fortunato said aloud for the second time, leaning his round body farther over the coffee table, closer to the mantel across the room. The most interesting thought of all was coming up. It was not one of the thoughts he had been thinking five nights a week for five years. Fortunato Alberto Lowe felt the new thought before he thought it. Then he thought it: buoyant fortieth birthday thought.

Of all the men in Lexington, Kentucky, Fortunato, himself, was the most likely to be visited by the Devil, himself.

Indeed, he had a very interesting mind. Perhaps, indeed, he was remarkably different from everybody else in Lexington, Kentucky.

And what was more—he had difficulty breathing over his finely different thought—he, Fortunato Lowe, was willing to list his non-Lexington qualities which warranted a visit from the Devil.

Although he played the stereo and attended the community concert series, he loathed music.

Although his mother had frowned on drinking, he drank every day of the world.

Although he belonged to the Church of the Good Shepherd, he believed in Hume.

Although his mother had called him long distance to tell him to think without ceasing, he spent every working day in utter thoughtlessness.

And, in addition, he visited the house on Broadway the first Monday of every month.

Fortunato had scooted so close to the edge of the couch that he was in danger of falling off. But he held to the couch cushion with his damp hands and leaned still closer to the laughing black face. The arm of the stereo finished the last *Canto Flamenco* and swung back to click the machine to silence; Fortunato was too excited to turn over the stack of records.

In the back of his mind he considered thinking about the house on Broadway—his visit was not due for another three weeks. He supposed he was the only Rotarian who knew the house so intimately; certainly he was the only one who called the owner Mother Shipton. It wasn't her real name, but it was a pleasantry, and she always laughed until her gums showed when he said, "Mother Shipton, I have come to visit your daughters."

But Fortunato's interesting mind was not interested in thinking about Mother Shipton's daughters, even though his own remarkable mother would have disapproved of the daughters even more than wine.

"And what is more . . ." He was speaking aloud in the quiet room. "I have always fancied the idea of selling my soul to . . ." He paused dramatically before he said, with great vigor and for the third time, "the Devil," and there was a knock at the door.

"Hume," Fortunato said, springing to his feet. It had been years since he had read Hume for the Centre College term paper. But he could no more be sure than Hume that someone waited outside. "Billiard," Fortunato said, straightening his tie. "Balls," he said, smoothing his shirt front. If a man didn't hear a step on the stair, a man had a right to assume that only a spirit waited behind the knock. "Ergo," Fortunato said, moving to the door. True, the stairs were carpeted, but he should have heard the elevator doors bang. They had awakened him at six this very morning. He had meant to put in a complaint on his way in, but the banging doors had slipped his interesting mind.

"The romance of Central Kentucky at dinner, indeed," Fortunato said, feeling a sharp twitch of pity for his poor deluded father. He swung the door open so wholeheartedly that the knob gouged the wallpaper.

"How do you do?" he said before he really saw the man.

He was of medium height, dark, balding, with a leather folder under his arm. He was an anonymous type man, worthy of the Devil, who had to look different for different people. Fortunato thought for a breath, just the instant of a rapid breath, that the man resembled his own mother. Mary Lowe had dressed up at Halloween and played her accordion at the P.T.A. carnivals until Fortunato was out of University High. It would have been just like her to masquerade as a businessman Devil with a slim briefcase under her arm and a surprised look on her face.

"You are the Devil I don't believe in," Fortunato said to himself, and aloud he said, "Come right in."

The man said Mr. Lowe's name questioningly. Fortunato was positive the visitor spoke his name.

"Come right on in," Fortunato said as cordially as his mother herself would have said it, and the man was sitting in the gray chair, his back to the mantel, and Fortunato had fetched the spare bottle from the refrigerator. "Plenty, plenty," the man said after his tumbler had received two gurgles, and Fortunato said, "Perhaps you prefer Bourbon."

"Wine is fine," the man said.

"And candy's dandy," Fortunato said, his mind knife sharp, and they were drinking together and smiling at each other as if they were very old friends.

Their camaraderie had happened quicker than you could say Jack Robinson. In fact, Fortunato was under the impression that the man said his name was Jack Robinson, which proved he wasn't from Lexington. The town was full of Robinsons, but no Jacks. But everything happened so quickly at first that Fortunato was a trifle confused, despite his sharp mind.

"You are new here?" Fortunato asked, leaning back on the couch so that the visitor's head blocked the mantel. He wasn't going to run the risk of having his mind further diverted by the image in the marble.

"Several years." The man smiled.

It was possible he was telling the truth. Fortunato knew every businessman in Lexington; it was his business to know every businessman. But the visitor could have been connected with the University of Kentucky. "University?"

"Oh no." The man was a jolly Devil. He laughed as if Fortunato had made a splendid joke. The man's laughter was flattering. Almost nobody except Mother Shipton considered Fortunato a wit.

"I see." He did not see at all, but he was gracious. His mother always said that Fortunato had the Hunt graciousness, at least in business matters. This was obviously business. Fortunato had made everybody in Central Kentucky understand, graciously of course, that his apartment was not to be invaded for social trifles.

"Nice place you have here."

Fortunato said, "Thank you," and relaxed. A man had to pretend that a business call was social for a while. This was a Lexington truth he had learned as a child from Cousin Martha Smith. She always left her card, even when she went to the bank to borrow money. It was thoroughly natural, then, that the visitor should go through the usual October talk before he got around to the business of soul-bartering. The paragraph on weather would be followed by the paragraph on football and another on the Keeneland racetrack.

Fortunato read the sports page of the *Leader* carefully enough to talk knowingly. "Did you get out to Keeneland?" he asked, hurrying the conference a little. But he was honestly relaxed, and it was amusing to entertain the Devil unaware. It was all as different as Mary Lowe could have wished. And the conversation ran as smoothly as if by telephone. Fortunato Lowe was a master of the telephone conversation, if he did say so himself.

"Another drop?" Fortunato asked.

"I don't care if I do," the man said, and they were through with the preliminaries.

"What I wanted to ask you about . . ." the man began, unzipping one side of his folder.

"I discussed football and racing with you only to be polite. I do not care for any sports. I gave up attending years ago. I despise music, Spanish dances, first, and then anything played on the accordion." Fortunato spoke slowly emphasizing every syllable in an interesting manner. He was hypnotizing the Devil, he was obviously hypnotizing the Devil. "I do demand beauty in women. Mother Shipton's daughters are not in the least beautiful. I do not respect the memory of Henry Clay, or Cousin Martha Smith, or my father, or John Hunt Morgan. I even dislike fresh air. Although I attend . . ."

The Devil interrupted with a phrase: "Great, oh man," or "Credo of man." Fortunato could not be sure which, but he was sure the Devil was delighted. He was smiling broadly. He lowered his hand, and he said quite distinctly, "I'm telling you."

"I'm telling you," Fortunato said.

"You really were," the visitor said, and he began to laugh appreciatively. "You sure enough are," his face remained white, despite the unselfish laughter which boiled and bubbled in his throat. The visitor's white laughter was infinitely preferable to Wallace C. Lowe's red-faced variety.

Fortunato wanted to laugh, too, but he didn't allow himself, not yet. "I'm telling you," Fortunato repeated and then he stopped short. "One example is worth a hundred generalizations. You agree?"

"I couldn't agree more." The Devil chortled. Fortunato didn't know when he had heard a chortle. It was his mother's favorite word, and here the Devil was chortling like anything.

"I'm telling you a secret I promised not to think about. I haven't even thought about it for five full years."

"Please, please," the visitor said.

Fortunato Alberto Lowe dampened his lips with his tongue. He was excited, in a way, but he was calm, too. It was all very interesting. And he was already so amused by his own story that he knew he was going to have trouble getting it out. He had never dreamed it would be so difficult to keep a straight face in front of the Devil. "My mother said to me, 'Fortunato Alberto, you must think all of the time but you must never think about this. Promise your dying mother.' Those are her very words."

The Devil reached into his hip pocket for a handkerchief. He wiped at the tears in his light eyes. "Go on, go on," he said helplessly, leaning over the coffee table so that he would not miss a word.

"She commanded me to bring the trunk which housed her collection of chiffon flowers. She had the world's greatest collection." Fortunato knew that his nose was twitching, but he was holding up—his voice was holding up splendidly. "She told me in a whisper that she had always considered chiffon flowers unattractive and foreign to her type of beauty. She said that my father hated them, too. 'Therefore,' said my mother, 'I considered them worthy of collection. As a community leader I considered them worthy.'"

"Oh, God," the Devil said, which was very charming of him.

Fortunato would have liked to tell the story in minute detail, but he knew he could not last through the details. As surely as he was a food broker, he was going to be struck with the giggles, and it was enormously important to get the story recorded for the visitor's ears.

"She . . . she made me burn every petal in the fireplace of Cousin Martha's bedroom with all the curlicues, the fireplace, I mean. It was my mother's bedroom at the time, I mean."

"Please. No," said the visitor, holding his side.

"Every single petal." Fortunato deliberately turned his eyes away from his guest. He couldn't look at the convulsed man and finish the story. In the mantel his own face grinned blackly. His mother's face was not in the mantel, which made the story twice as funny. "Five years ago," he gasped, "she died . . . laughing."

"No, no, no," the Devil said rocking back and forth.

"That's my heritage, Sir. Now . . ." But there was no point in trying to hold back any longer. Fortunato copied his guest and pressed his own handkerchief against his mouth. But the whinnies of laughter escaped the handkerchief to blend with the visitor's deeper guffaws. He wanted to tell the Devil that they were laughing a duet, but the words were too funny to utter.

Fortunato was not drunk, of course. It took more than a little wine to make him drunk. But he allowed himself the luxury of pretending to be drunk. He sloshed drinks for himself and his delightful companion, and lurched back to the couch, deliberately crashing his elbow against the tune arm of the stereo, scratching the *Canto Flamenco* permanently. His actions were so humorous that he feared for a moment that his guest would collapse.

"I've told you all this," Fortunato managed to gasp. "I've told you all this because . . ." He had to beat his fists on his knees. "Because I wanted to put all my cards on the table, and . . ." He knew he was going to be so funny that the visitor couldn't stand it. "I don't like cards."

"I can't stand it," the Devil said, as Fortunato knew he would.

"It's my birthday," Fortunato said.

"Happy birthday," the man roared, and they were off again.

It was the visitor who got control of himself first, naturally, since he had first lost control. "You're the limit," he said, finally, when the laughter in him had subsided to a mere boiling point.

"Please, no," Fortunato said.

"I've heard about you, but I never dreamed," the man said, wiping his eyes finally with his wet handkerchief.

For a moment, only for a moment, Fortunato's flesh actually crawled. It moved like worms over his hands and arms and shoulders. For a moment he wondered if the visitor were local instead of universal. He wondered if the visitor could be some young upstart fresh out of the College of Commerce selling insurance or cemetery lots. The visitor's bland face, fresh washed by his hilarious tears, looked foolishly young. He looked young enough to be fresh out of the College of Commerce.

"You're the Devil," Fortunato said.

"You said it," the young man said.

"I knew. I knew all the time." Fortunato lifted his hand to his face as if to feel a veil. He felt only flesh. He could not imagine why he had been so amused.

"You're one in a million," the man said.

"I'm as relaxed as a chiffon flower." Fortunato leaned his head back against the couch. "What am I offered?" he asked aloud against the darkness of his eyelids. "I'm willing to sell my soul as sure as my name is Fortunato Alberto Lowe."

"Your name is different all right," the sober voice of the visitor answered. "For Lexington."

Fortunato did not say, "I'm different for anywhere." He said, instead, "You're buying?"

In the midst of the darkness Fortunato heard the sound of two zips. With the closing of the briefcase he heard the movement of his own mind, as real as the flutter of sparrow wings against a pongee curtain.

Fortunato remained calm. He did not open his eyes although he knew, as true as billiard balls, that the interview was over. The room as quiet as a cork.

Time had always been long enough—waiting for the busy signal to turn to a dial tone, or for the chiffon petals to burn, or for Mother Shipton's daughters to get ready. Time had always been plenty long enough. Still, for propriety's sake, it was important to play out the scene.

"I'm one in a million," Fortunato said, wishing it were so.

"That's right," the Devil said politely.

"I'm the limit," Fortunato said, wishing again.

"Sure. Of course."

"I would have sold quite cheap, you know."

The young man's voice sounded very tired. "Yeah," he said. "So would everybody else."

Fortunato opened his eyes. "I wish you had shown me the certificates, and the seals, anyhow."

"You know what they're like."

"But you came." Fortunato stood up. "At least you came."

"You said it right," the Devil said, extending his soft hand.

"Goodnight, Sir," Fortunato said. He had tried to sell his soul to the Devil he didn't believe in and the Devil wouldn't buy. But it was all right, as the man said.

"Good-bye, Mr. Lowell," the Devil said, and he was out of the door as quietly as a puff of smoke.

"Lowe, Fortu . . ."

Fortunato watched the closed door of his apartment until he heard the clang of the elevator doors. The Devil was a stupid man, for all his charm and graciousness.

"Everybody in Lexington, Kentucky," Fortunato said, and he sat down on the couch again.

He looked at the mantel out of the corner of his eye, at first, then full face. His remarkable mother was there, all right. "I'm sorry," Fortunato said.

"It's all right?" Fortunato said.

"It's all right," a voice said almost simultaneously.

Fortunato reached for the last of the wine which he believed in for his stomach's sake. There was still a nice sized drink in the bottle. It was warm, but it was a nice sized drink.

He turned over the stack of records on the stereo.

In a little while he would go to the bathroom and brush his teeth. He would set the alarm for 6:15, a half hour earlier than usual. He would stop at the hotel desk on his way to work to complain about the elevator doors. He could not afford to be waked so early as he had been on his birthday morning. A man needed his rest if he were going to carry on the business he believed in.

The Vireo's Nest

THE RUSTIC slab at the entrance to the camp said Artist's Colony of Kentucky. On either side of the word *Kentucky* stood a stylized mountain. The sign had been painted in neat thin letters by a girl who, ten years later, was given a show at the Mexican-American Cultural Institute as well as the Sharonville Public Library. That is why Dr. Thornton, the founder and director of the colony, kept the sign. Even though the artists were all writers now, they didn't mind being called artists. They frequently talked about the girl who had painted the sign, although few could recall her name.

As usual the prospectus and the actuality of the colony were several degrees apart. Bill Moore, the instructor in short story and poetry, said the promise and the reality were light years apart. But Bill Moore was twenty-four and fresh out of the University of Kentucky with a Master's degree and a privately published volume of verse. Dr. Thornton's A.C.K. bulletin, *Mountain Breeze*, had quieted considerably through the years. In 1940 when the colony was founded, he had announced Ernest Hemingway as a faculty member, merely because Ernest Hemingway had been invited.

This year his instructional staff of three were all present: Dr. Eloise Delgado, a professor of biology from Louisville, returning for her seventh summer; Dr. Thornton himself, who conducted the essay workshop in addition to his other duties; and young Bill Moore.

Dr. Delgado was in charge of the nature walks as well as the craft hour. She was a tall woman with beautiful snow-white hair. Janice Watts and Bill Moore kept telling each other that she was a dead ringer for a snowy crested crane. Neither Janice nor Bill was an authority on bird life; they were not even sure that the snowy crested crane existed, but they enjoyed their joke and giggled together at dinner every time Mrs. Titelbaum, of Philadelphia, announced her discovery of another rare specimen. Mrs. Titelbaum was al-

46

ways seeing exotic birds previously unknown to the mountains of Kentucky. Miss Delgado was very patient with her.

"Snowy crested crane?" Janice whispered to Bill. Janice was from Knoxville, and only eighteen. Her parents were doing Europe.

"No private jokes," Dr. Thornton said from the head of the table whenever Janice and Bill took a giggling fit.

But the twenty ladies of the colony were sympathetic with the young people. "Leave them alone," someone would say, and Mrs. Titelbaum always remarked that you were only young once, take it from her, Grandma Moses. Mrs. Titelbaum liked to refer to herself as the Grandma Moses of literature. She was working on a history of Philadelphia.

Even Mary Scott defended the young people in her own quiet way. "It's good to laugh," she said the fourth evening she was at the colony. It was an interesting thing for her to say, because nobody had seen her laugh, up to and including that moment. She smiled, yes, but she was a strange one. She had been a week late for the June session. She was Mrs. Scott and she came clear from Texas; she had no children. She said she had read Dr. Thornton's announcement in a writers' magazine, but she didn't volunteer the story of her life the way everybody else did. Mrs. Titelbaum was offended by Mary Scott at first, which was unfortunate since Mary's cabin was right next door in Circle One. But when Mrs. Titelbaum discovered, after careful questioning, that Mary's husband had died only a month ago, she took it upon herself to protect the young widow. Mrs. Titelbaum felt terribly bad over Mary's loss. She had lost three husbands herself, but not by death.

The evening Mary Scott said, "It's good to laugh," Bill and Janice took their usual walk along Meditation Path, from the lodge to beyond Circle One. In the midst of their customary and spirited kissing in the shadows, Bill told Janice he couldn't endure the colony if it weren't for their little walks together. Already the bell for Inspiration sounded. Bill said, "God damn," again and again into Janice's ear. The words tasted like food. He wished he dared to shout "God damn," at the meeting. "God damn Thornton," Bill said.

"Please, please, honey." Janice rubbed her hand up and down Bill's neck. In her right hand she held her flashlight. Everybody carried a flashlight after sunset, but Janice's was the only one decorated with jewels. "Honey." Bill's hair was coarse, and she was head over heels in love with him. She knew it positively.

"Him and his spiritual emphasis," Bill said brokenly. Dr. Thornton thought positively in all directions. Dr. Thornton boasted that the Artist's Colony was the only non-alcoholic writers' center in the world. Dr. Thornton said the mountain air was more intoxicating than any beverage.

"Honey, honey, sweet." Janice dropped her flashlight, but, fortunately, it was uninjured. "Write a poem about it. Write a poem and get it out of your system. Sweet, sweet." She thought of herself as Elizabeth Barrett to Robert.

It was a fine moment for the two of them.

But walking back to the lodge, hand in hand, their breathing almost normal again, Bill said, "That Mary Scott, I like her looks."

"All right, I guess." Janice shrugged her plump shoulders.

"She's smooth. And she's the only woman here under ninety—except you, of course."

"She hasn't bought your book yet," Janice said. She thought of letting go of Bill's hand, but decided against it. Every other member of the colony had purchased Bill's volume the day the session opened. Several had even sent to Louisville for copies of Dylan Thomas and Walter Benton on Bill's recommendation.

"What's buying a book? What's money?" Frequently Bill spoke against money, although he knew that Janice was an honest to goodness heiress.

"You be careful, or I'll get jealous." She yanked her hand away, scraping her large diamond dinner ring against the flesh of Bill's hand. She hoped she had hurt him.

"Baby, baby," Bill said, realizing that the conversation was clear out of hand, and realizing anew how much the Meditation Walks meant to him. "She's forty if she's a day. Look at me, sweetheart."

Mary Scott was not forty. She was only thirty-four.

Janice and Bill embraced again, dangerously near Circle Five and Pegasus—the lodge which was the heart of A.C.K.: dining room, classroom, conference room, and quarters for Dr. Thornton. "Hmmmm," Janice said, and Bill said, "Once more," as the last gong for Inspiration beat wildly against their ears. They strained against each other and it was Janice who muttered, "God damn."

But they were not the last to arrive at Pegasus. Dr. Thornton tapped a pencil on the table. "Where's Mrs. Titelbaum?" he asked crossly, and then, more gently, "We don't want anybody to miss anything." Dr. Thornton looked hard through his little pig eyes at Bill Moore. In spite of himself Bill offered to run up to Mrs. Titelbaum's cabin.

"Never mind. We'll wait three more minutes." Dr. Thornton turned his head slowly to smile at each individual member of the colony, including Bill. A thousand times Dr. Thornton had been told his smile was captivating. "Hypnotic, even," one woman said three seasons ago.

The Inspiration was composed of music and readings. Dr. Thornton owned a very fine record player and a collection of the complete works of Tchaikovsky as well as other favorites. If the members of the colony failed to bring original work, the records were played. Dr. Thornton was fond of saying that truly great music forced language from the soul. "Listen tonight and you'll have reams of original work for tomorrow night," Dr. Thornton said, even if nobody had brought any original work for three days.

"Do we all have something to read tonight?" Dr. Thornton asked when the three minutes were up. It was really four minutes and ten seconds. Mrs. Titelbaum had still not appeared.

Bill had brought a poem—an old poem he'd written in Lexington, but he didn't dare appear without something. "I have a new little piece," he said, and three of the ladies applauded.

"I have another chapter of my Benny the Bug," the woman from Horse Cave said.

One lady had at last finished her personal experience paragraph which was due in Dr. Thornton's class a week ago.

Dr. Thornton leaned back in his chair. "This is more like it," he said, smiling until his eyes actually disappeared.

But the original work was destined to be postponed for another evening.

Mrs. Titelbaum began calling before she reached the porch. "Everybody! Everybody, quick!"

Dr. Thornton tried very hard to be a patient executive. Many people often spoke of his patience. He had never allowed anything to disrupt the Inspirations—they were the proof of the pudding, he often said so. But he had never had Mrs. Titelbaum as a colony member before.

"I've found a vireo's nest," Mrs. Titelbaum shouted, waving her unlit railroad lantern back and forth. Mrs. Titelbaum owned the largest light in the colony. "I've really found a vireo's nest."

Miss Delgado lifted her long white neck. "Really? I've been searching for one all summer."

"Really and truly. In Circle One. In *our* cluster of cabins." She looked accusingly at Miss Delgado, and then she looked accusingly at Bill Moore.

Janice Watts turned her head. Janice lived in Circle Four with her aunt—she was positive that Dr. Thornton had placed her as far as possible from Bill on purpose. Janice did not want Mrs. Titelbaum to look accusingly at her. She was sorry, for a moment, that she had laughed every time Mrs. Titelbaum had announced a new bird.

"If you don't believe it, come see."

Miss Delgado was rising, and so was Mary Scott.

"A vireo's nest," Mary Scott said quietly. She liked the sound of the words.

"If we don't go now, there won't be enough light," Miss Delgado said. "We will not use our torches on the nest." She spoke with authority. Janice removed her finger from the pearl button of her flashlight.

Dr. Thornton started to tell them to keep their seats. But five more ladies rose, and then three. Dr. Thornton had to raise his voice to announce: "Our Inspiration this evening will be devoted to a lecture on the vireo from Dr. Delgado." There was nothing else he could say. "Remember—tomorrow night—everybody—everybody with a manuscript."

Dr. Thornton took two little skipping steps to get to the front of the group. He was angry. Anybody would have been angry. But he was a patient man. And it was important for the colony members to realize that he was, likewise, a man of flexibility.

There really was a bird's nest in the maple tree which stood smack dab in the center of Circle One. Janice would have to admit it was a vireo's nest, a red-eyed vireo. Miss Delgado said so, and Miss Delgado knew everything. You could almost see the little greenish grayish thing sitting there; you could almost see its red eye. Everybody stood very quietly in front of Bill's cabin, and learned everything there was to know about the vireo—its sex life, and everything. Bill stood very close behind Janice. She wished she had found the nest as a present for Bill. It was really a darling nest: it was shaped like an egg itself, and it hung there, not six feet from the ground, right in the fork of some little tiny twigs.

Janice could have found the nest if she hadn't been so excited over that Bill Moore. She'd waited in front of his cabin a dozen times while he went in to get something. She didn't know why she couldn't get up the nerve to go in the cabin herself. Sometimes she just couldn't figure herself out.

Janice Watts leaned hard against Bill. And the rascal was moving his hands against her back. He was really kneading her back. Miss Delgado kept talking in her sweet voice which wouldn't scare a bird. Miss Delgado would say just anything. She was saying something about "crotch" now; she was saying, "the crotch of the tree."

Miss Delgado gave a rather long lecture, for she was an authority on the vireo, at least the twelve vireos of the United States. She mentioned the tropical vireos only in passing. "They feed chiefly on insects. They devour worms, insects, and their larvae," she said in the same voice in which she had spoken of mating habits. "Like the flycatcher, they are capable of snatching insects on the wing." Miss Delgado was not sure, but she thought the author of Benny the Bug winced.

She spoke until there was no more daylight. Again she cautioned the colony members against throwing the beams of their lights into the nest. Dr. Thornton announced that from now on they would start their nature walks at the nest of the red-eyed vireo. "Operation Vireo," Dr. Thornton said, and they were dismissed to go to their cabins and write, write, write.

Benny the Bug asked Bill for a manuscript conference up at Pegasus. There was nothing Bill could do but go with her. There was nothing for Janice Watts to do but go to her cabin and write, write, write. She wished to hell her parents had let her come to the conference alone. Her great-aunt Anna Jane wore wool socks to bed and walked with a cane. Janice didn't speak to Aunt Anna Jane any more than absolutely necessary, so she managed a good bit of rewriting on the first chapter of her novel about the Knoxville Country Club set. The book was going to be something like *Bonjour Tristesse*, only Tennessee.

Mary Scott took comfort from the vireos. Even though the rains started the morning after Mrs. Titelbaum's discovery, Mary visited the nest at least a dozen times a day. She stood like a tree in the rain and watched. It was good

51

to think about the vireos, male and female, who resembled each other. It was good to anticipate their young—Miss Delgado had promised that the young would be "diminutive adults." Mary Scott did not brood over her childlessness, but she liked to think about the vireo family. The four white eggs, speckled with brown and black, looked the way eggs should look. Mary Scott tried to smile in the rain. Then she went back to her cabin to write letters.

She did not try to write anything but letters. Mary Scott had given up her little poems a long time ago—when Thomas first got sick. She had come to Kentucky to get away from the house where Thomas had breathed painfully for so long. She thought about Thomas almost all the time, but she did not talk about him except on rare occasions to Mrs. Titelbaum, poor soul, who needed confidences.

Everyone was kind in the colony. They all assured Mary Scott that the rain was very unusual. Mary Scott tried not to mind the rain. Still, her underclothes were clammy, her towels stayed damp, and the mushrooms sprouted scarlet and orange around her cabin. After the third day of the deluge, she had the ridiculous feeling that the mushrooms were stationary and she was dwindling, like Alice in Wonderland. On occasion, the scarlet eye of the vireo itself loomed monstrous. Mary included the *Alice* notion in all of her letters. She wrote her friends at home, and she wrote Thomas' family in the east. The dampness made the shift key on her typewriter sluggish, creating capital letters where none were intended. "I'M NOt angry," she wrote her mother in Houston. "IT'S Only this machine." She was taken with the idea of a typewriter with a mind of its own, and carefully included the sentences in a number of letters.

After a week the sun came out. Mary Scott knew the sun was out before she opened her eyes.

"Good morning, good morning, good morning," Mrs. Titelbaum called at the door. "Time to visit our babies."

Mary Scott had overslept. She could not remember when she had overslept before. For a moment she felt guilty. For a moment she wondered if Thomas had needed her.

"A minute. Just a couple of minutes."

Thomas had not needed her, of course. Thomas was dead. Mary Scott had waited on her husband for a year and a half. Then she had given him the

52

extra tablets. Thomas said, "Thank you, Mary." Thomas said, "I love you, Mary."

Mary Scott looked at her eyes in the bubbled mirror over the washstand. For a moment she remembered the vireo's eyes.

Mrs. Titelbaum accompanied her to the bathhouse. She talked about the birds while Mary bathed her face in cold water. Mrs. Titelbaum began to remember birds in Philadelphia as Mary took her damp towel from the rod with her name over it. Dr. Thornton had done the lettering himself. Everything at A.C.K. was as carefully arranged as a kindergarten. "You're a dear," Mary told Mrs. Titelbaum, and the last breakfast bell began to ring.

Mrs. Titelbaum had been a little hurt when Miss Delgado said the red-eyed vireo was the commonest vireo in North America. She did not like to think of her birds as common. But now, now that the vireos were out, actually out . . . Well! She couldn't have been more delighted if she had laid and hatched them herself. Bill told her she was nothing but a mother vireo. Mrs. Titelbaum laughed as loudly as any of the group standing at a respectful distance from the maple tree. "Just look at them. God love their souls," Mrs. Titelbaum said, and Bill said, "See, I told you."

At dinner Dr. Thornton said that Mother Nature herself was concerned with the entertainment of the colony members. Janice said she still wished she had found the nest. Miss Delgado said, "Why, Janice!" Miss Delgado took the birth of the babies in her stride, but you could tell she was as pleased as anyone. "It's just you're used to Nature," Mrs. Titelbaum told her. Miss Delgado smiled serenely. The author of Benny the Bug asked the group what they thought of the idea of changing her title to Benny the Vireo. Mrs. Titelbaum was so excited over the idea that her eyes were moist.

Then—it was on a Friday, after lunch—one of the vireo babies got off the nest. It was the baby which Mrs. Titelbaum had named after herself—she was positive it was the same one. Janice found the little thing hopping through the brush by Bill's cabin. She had slipped up the back way to Circle One, determined this time to walk right up to Bill's door, to reach out her hand, to turn the knob—nobody ever locked a door at the Artist's Colony of Kentucky—and walk in. She hadn't planned exactly what she would do after she walked in.

But when she saw the vireo, she shouted. Mrs. Titelbaum, whose subcon-

53

scious was keeping twenty-four-hour vigil over the nest, was at her cabin door in a flash. "I knew when I heard Janice Watts scream that something was wrong with the babies," Mrs. Titelbaum told each person who arrived at the scene. It was amazing how many colony members congregated. Even Janice's Aunt Anna Jane was there, cane and all. But Aunt Anna Jane had been on her way for some time. She had sensed that Janice was headed for Bill's cabin although she wouldn't have admitted it, not to a living soul.

Mary Scott stood behind the chattering group, feeling as detached as if she were a cloud. She had been writing to Thomas' father. Inadvertently she had written W.C. for Writers' Conference. She laughed aloud as she took the paper from the typewriter. You didn't write W.C. in a letter to Thomas' father, even if you meant Writers' Conference.

Dr. Thornton didn't appear at all because he was conducting his essay workshop up at Pegasus. His enrollment was down to three. Bill Moore slept through the whole confusion.

Mrs. Titelbaum was trying to scoop the baby into her rebosa when Miss Delgado sailed through the trees. For all her quiet ways, Miss Delgado's voice carried well. "Back. Back, everybody," she said, and everybody moved back. "The bird is to be left alone."

"I'm only trying to *put* him back," Mrs. Titelbaum said, and Janice identified the spot where she had first seen the baby; Benny's author said, "But he's so little," and Mrs. Titelbaum said, "I knew when I heard Janice Watts scream . . ."

"The fledglings are almost ready to fly," Miss Delgado said more quietly than ever. "The parents will attend to their own young."

"What if something happens to him?" Mrs. Titelbaum was already defeated, but she felt it her duty to argue.

"He will very likely grow to adulthood," Miss Delgado was almost whispering. "If, by chance, a snake or some other enemy . . ."

"Snake! My God!" Janice said.

"Janice Watts," Aunt Anna Jane said.

"But a snake!"

"Really, Miss Delgado." Mrs. Titelbaum placed her hand over her heart.

"I said he would very likely grow to adulthood." Miss Delgado stood taller

54

than ever. "One accepts the pattern of Nature." Her voice came close to being emotional.

"A snake," Mary Scott said, but not aloud. She felt she should be sharing the horror on Mrs. Titelbaum's face, but *snake* was only a word like *death*. It was only a word on a typewriter.

"I know you all have work awaiting you," Miss Delgado said.

Mrs. Titelbaum jerked her rebosa angrily around her shoulders. There was nothing to do but leave—not when Miss Delgado was determined to stand sentinel at the circle.

"They are without dignity," Miss Delgado said to herself as the women straggled away in their colored shoes, muttering to each other. She had seen a handsome black snake behind her cabin the day before yesterday and again this morning. She had frightened the snake away, of course. She had rapped her hairbrush against the screen. She had said, "Shoo," softly, so Mrs. Titelbaum next door would not hear. Almost every season there was a snake scare. Miss Delgado wondered, fleetingly, if she should have killed the animal and had it done with. But it had moved so beautifully. There was no movement more beautiful.

Miss Delgado was still standing at the edge of the circle when Bill opened his door. Bill Moore looked up at the sky, and yawned, and scratched his stomach with both hands. Then he saw Miss Delgado. She was not poised on one foot, but she gave that impression—it was the camouflage of sun through leaves.

"The parents were just coming," Miss Delgado said. She sounded sad rather than angry. Bill was sure she sounded sad. She explained about the little vireo. She said, "Hysterical women." Bill was sure he had heard her correctly. Then she shrugged her thin shoulders and crossed the clearing to her cabin. She did not even pause to look at the vireo's nest.

The parents did not get the baby. Dr. Thornton had great difficulty in settling the group for Inspiration. There were no manuscripts—he had anticipated that there would be no manuscripts: the camp was out of tune. He liked to think of himself as harpist, the members of the colony as strings. But the blasted vireo had nested in the mechanics of his instrument.

Dr. Thornton had chosen "Swan Lake" music and a Fritz Kreisler album

55

for the evening. It was unfortunate indeed that both albums were 78 revolutions, rather than 33. With the changing of each record someone—Mrs. Titelbaum or someone—would further untune the harp. "I just can't rest easy," Mrs. Titelbaum said, and "The poor little thing. The poor little baby."

Finally, after the last of the Kreisler numbers, he turned to Miss Delgado. He was going to ask her if something couldn't be done about the baby. Miss Delgado was really a very sensitive person. She seemed to anticipate his question. She turned her head slowly. Like a white flower on its stem, Dr. Thornton thought. He was suddenly struck by Miss Delgado's beauty. After seven sessions he was suddenly struck. "Remember, tomorrow night, manuscripts everybody," Dr. Thornton said, shattered by his own imagery.

None of the camp members ever saw the little vireo again. In fact, nobody except Mary Scott remembered him until the next morning after breakfast. Mary mentioned him to Mrs. Titelbaum, and Mrs. Titelbaum stopped at several cabins to discuss the poor little fellow. But by then it was too late for real mourning. All of their grief had been given to his three brothers, and the manuscript of Benny Vireo was already back to its original title. The author from Horse Cave had made the changes before the first breakfast bell.

Mrs. Titelbaum discovered the snake in the maple tree. She would always consider it the strangest thing in her entire life that it was she who discovered both the nest and the snake. She was returning from the bathhouse at ten o'clock. She was sure it was ten o'clock, because she had looked at her wrist watch in the dim light—you would have thought Dr. Thornton could have provided brighter bulbs for the bathhouse, at least. It was ten o'clock— she had thought it was nearer eleven.

As she headed across Circle One she turned her lantern into the tree. She did it deliberately. She even told Miss Delgado she had done it deliberately. And there was the snake. Its ugly face was right at the crotch of the birds' branch. He was stretching himself along the limb toward the nest. "Slowly, slowly, slowly," Mrs. Titelbaum said. She held her light on the snake—she'd never know why she didn't drop the lantern—and she screamed at the top of her voice. She screamed and screamed until almost everybody in the colony was there. She couldn't stop screaming.

Bill Moore and Janice Watts were the first ones. Mrs. Titelbaum was never so glad to see anybody in her life as she was Bill Moore. Janice had Anna

Jane's cane, which was a lucky thing, though what the child was doing with a cane nobody ever thought to ask. "Kill him. Kill the son of a bitch," Mrs. Titelbaum shouted at Bill.

The movement of the snake was almost hypnotic. There was a moon, and then there were the flashlights rushing against the darkness and flooding the trees. Bill Moore had never seen a snake in a tree before. He had almost never seen a snake except in the Cincinnati Zoo. For a moment he wished that all of this were happening an hour ago. It would have been splendidly ironic if Mrs. Titelbaum had screamed just as Janice came into his cabin. Janice had been giggling. "Aunt Anna Jane won't follow me tonight," she said before Bill reached up to unscrew the center bulb.

"Do! Do something! Do something!" Mrs. Titelbaum's voice was ragged with fear.

"Rocks. Get rocks," Benny's author chanted. "Rocks."

"We must surround him," Bill said.

"Not yet. Wait. Wait." Dr. Thornton was breathing so heavily that it was painful to form words, but he had to speak. "Let him get to the nest before you strike." He filled his lungs with air. "We'll have a better chance if he gets to the nest."

Janice Watts began to cry. Her jeweled flashlight shook with her sobs.

"No," Miss Delgado said quietly. She wore a dark quilted bathrobe; her beautiful white hair hung loose over her shoulders. She moved past the semi-circle of watchers into the glare of lights. She lifted her hand to the branch. The snake stopped.

"It stopped and looked at her, I'll swear it did," Mrs. Titelbaum was to say every time she told the story in Philadelphia. "She told us never to touch the tree even, and there she was reaching up for the nest."

"It's empty," Miss Delgado said. "I was afraid it would be."

"Then she touched the snake's head with her long thin fingers," Mrs. Titelbaum would say. And no matter how many times she told the story, she shivered every time she came to the part about Miss Delgado's touching the snake's head.

Mary Scott had seen snakes before. Once on her father's ranch in Texas a rattler had killed a horse. And once, running through a wheat field, with some psychic knowledge she had jumped clear of a coiled rattler. But this

57

was no rattler. He made no sound as he moved smoothly back along the branch, retreating from the cool fingers of a white-haired woman in a quilted robe. He was only a black snake, and there was no sound from anything. Mary remembered herself as a child, running with the wind. She had not thought of herself as a child for a long long time.

Someone threw a stone, barely missing Miss Delgado's head.

Mary remembered the other vireo, lost now, she was sure. "The red eye of the vireo," she said to herself without fear.

Janice Watts hiccoughed, and the spell of quiet was broken. Miss Delgado turned away from the tree. "If we only had a gun," Bill Moore said. "Everyone be very careful, very careful," Dr. Thornton's breath was as loud as his words. "The nasty thing," Janice sobbed.

Mary Scott placed her flashlight on the ground. She moved to Janice Watts's side. She took the cane from Janice's limp hand. She counted the steps it took her to reach the tree. One, two, three, four, five. Then she swung at the snake's head. She felt the head give. She was conscious that her mouth moved with each stroke, almost as if she were still counting. She swung again and again. She swung, finally, with such force that she herself fell, scraping her arm against the stones of the path.

Mrs. Titelbaum began to applaud, and someone shouted, "Hurrah," and then they were around her, pulling at her. "Leave me alone," she said against her hands. "Please leave me alone."

Miss Delgado picked up the cane from the path. Almost as if in ritual, she lifted the snake's glistening body onto the cane. "It was a beauty," Miss Delgado said to anyone who was listening. "It is easily five feet long."

"Seven. It's seven feet," someone said.

"I'm all right. I'm all right, I tell you," Mary Scott said.

Miss Delgado placed the snake under the tree. "Stones," she said efficiently, and several of the women brought stones, stretching their arms to hand them to Miss Delgado. Efficiently she began to place a little pile on the pulp which had been the snake's head.

Mrs. Titelbaum got Mary Scott to her feet. "Poor baby," she said. "Poor courageous baby."

Mary Scott tried to laugh. But when she saw Miss Delgado, the laugh broke.

She leaned against the rough bark of Miss Delgado's cabin. She pressed her hands behind her, hard against the rough bark. She was all right. She was really all right. She could talk about the snake. She could already talk about the snake. "When I was a child, the Mexicans used to take a stick and gouge the head into the ground," she told Mrs. Titelbaum who clucked behind her. "I couldn't do that."

"Of course you couldn't." Mrs. Titelbaum bravely held back her tears. "Of course not." Never would anybody hear the songs of her red-eyed vireos singing through the hot days of August. "Of course, of course."

"We could slit his stomach open maybe and save the poor little birds," Janice Watts said, approaching Miss Delgado. Bill Moore held Janice's elbow, standing a little behind her. He wanted to say something, but he couldn't think of anything to say.

"Nonsense," Miss Delgado said, beginning a pile of stones on the tail.

Bill turned his head away. Mary Scott was watching him. She was either watching him or staring into space. For a moment he thought about dancing with Mary Scott. It was only the sudden turning of his head which made him think of dancing. He was sorry he was so mixed up with Janice. It would have been fine, really fine, if Mary Scott were his friend. If he and Mary Scott went to bed together . . .

Bill lowered his eyes. He couldn't look at Mary Scott. It was funnier than hell how he felt, here, now, squeezing Janice's elbow. He would speak to Mary Scott, of course. He and Mary Scott would talk together up at Pegasus. But that would be all. It was a god damned shame. It was god damned ridiculous. It was god damned ridiculous to feel this way, as if Mary Scott were the god damned sun and you couldn't look at her but for a second.

"It's moving. It's moving," Janice screamed.

Bill thought so too. He held Janice's elbow tighter than ever.

"Muscular reaction," Miss Delgado said, adding another stone.

Dr. Thornton clapped his hands together. "We're going to have coffee up at Pegasus," he shouted. "We'll wake the cook and have coffee and doughnuts. How does that sound?"

"It sounds just wonderful," Janice said, turning her round wet face up to Bill. "We'll go get Aunt Anna Jane."

They were all delighted over the thought of coffee and doughnuts. They squealed, but only for a moment. Already they were quieting. They linked arms. Already some of them were moving away from the Circle. Already their voices were as relaxed as if they were leaving church, or an evening of television.

"First, we'll sterilize the cane," Bill said. He spoke more loudly than he had intended, but it didn't matter. Several of the ladies said it was a very good idea.

"Our heroine should lead the way," Dr. Thornton said. "Where's our heroine?"

"Here she is. Right here," Mrs. Titelbaum said proudly.

Mary did not lean against the cabin. She stood very straight.

"Not tonight," Mary said. She smiled, almost shyly. It was god damned ridiculous to have thought of her face as the sun. "I don't think so tonight."

"She should get to bed, poor dear. Of course she should." Mrs. Titelbaum scowled at Dr. Thornton. She put her arm around Mary's waist.

Janice's foolish face was scowling, too. "What if there should be more snakes? Oh, Bill, what if there are more?"

Mary Scott cleared her throat. "There probably won't be any more, Janice," she said.

"Exactly." Miss Delgado rose from her twin monuments.

"They aren't very dangerous," Mary Scott said, looking straight at Miss Delgado. "They have no hands for protection—only a small mouth."

"That is very true, Mrs. Scott," Miss Delgado said.

For a moment Mary was afraid she was going to cry.

Later, after Mrs. Titelbaum had tiptoed out of Mary's cabin to join the coffee and doughnut party, Mary slipped a pair of slacks and a sweater over her pajamas. The snake was barely visible in the light of the clouded moon. It lay like the shadow of a maple limb between Miss Delgado's little rock piles.

Mary Scott walked over the whole camp, clear down to the highway and back again. She used her flashlight only a few times. It was surprising how well she had learned the camp, and anyhow, there was the moon. At the entrance she did flash her light for a glance at the sign with the stylized mountains. She tried to recall the name of the artist, but the name wouldn't come.

"Thomas," she said once, but only once.

Dolly

AFTER SHE had washed the little clothes in the upstairs bathroom, with the blinds close drawn and the door carefully fastened, she went downstairs and spread a towel in front of the gas grate and smoothed the pants, the slip, the organdy dress, the sweater, the frilled bonnet onto the towel. Then she lit the gas grate, even though it was May. She folded her arms and looked down at the clothes, dark because of their dampness, waiting for the heat.

She did not mean to tiptoe to the front door with its carved wood and beveled glass, but it was hard to keep from tiptoeing in the empty house. She opened the door only a fraction, and the honeysuckle which her mother had planted years and years ago pressed itself against the house. She closed her eyes and stood very straight before the narrow column of honeysuckle fragrance. Almost without consciousness she swung open the door and stepped out to the wide porch. The terraced yard dipped from the porch three times before it reached the brick sidewalk and the hot, new asphalt street. The yards of the Herricks and the Breckenridges which completed their side of the block dipped, too, like waves. On the other side of the asphalt stood the seven new houses; not new, exactly—perhaps it was eleven years ago that the Crawfords had started to build the last of the houses. It must have been eleven years ago; they were already working on the skeleton of the Crawford house the day she married Lewis and Pappa had told the builder, whatever his name was, that they would have to cease that infernal racket—that's what Pappa had said, "Cease that infernal racket."

She moved down the steps, clear down the third wave, and turned her body, which pressed against the black silk dress, to the houses on the street. The Breckenridges and the Herricks were asleep now, quite asleep, just as she had told them to be, their houses dark: "Please, please, no, I don't need anyone, not anyone at all, I'd rather stay by myself, I'm telling you the truth,

I'd really rather," she had said, and old Mrs. Breckenridge (Mamma would be as old as old Mrs. Breckenridge, now) and young Ellen—even the youngest Ellen was there, pulling at her mother's hand to get away from the house where the funeral smell still lingered—the two Ellens, and Tony Herrick and his wife, there were others but she could not remember their faces in the presence of the heavy honeysuckle, all of them, even the people on the other side of the street, had nodded and said together, like children chanting, "We understand," and they had all smiled at each other, as if they were children at a children's party, and she had felt quiet within the black silk dress which, she knew without vanity, utterly without vanity, made her youthful, desirable really, even to Lewis, particularly to Lewis, if Lewis were here, she would be desirable.

Only in the Crawfords' little house across the street burned a light. Mrs. Crawford had not said, "We understand," even though it was Mrs. Crawford who had been nice enough to wire her about Pappa's illness. Mrs. Crawford had moved through the house for three days now, washing dishes, and serving other people's food, and opening and closing cabinets as if she belonged in the house. Tomorrow, very early probably, round, young Mrs. Crawford would insist that she have lunch with them, she would not take *no* for an answer; her pink face would say, "It's no trouble at all; I can't bear to think about your being in that big house all day by yourself," and, "We may not be old friends, but we're good friends," and, "I loved your father; the Judge was the nicest old gentleman I ever knew, a real gentleman." And Mrs. Crawford would weep openly.

She turned and walked back into the house. She locked the door with the great brass key. She tried the door three times before she left the hall for the living room's light and heat. She sat carefully, bracing her hands on the green painted arms of the porch chair, as her father must have braced his hands when he sat for the last time. She would wait. She could wait. She would wait until Mrs. Crawford had finished putting her house to bed, "checking the children," she was forever checking the children, tidying up, as if her own house were one of her children, and then placing her round body beside the body of her sleeping husband who went early every morning into town to stand behind a bank's wicket. She could sense Mrs. Crawford's movements across the street, even as she sat as still as her father had sat when she had come out to see if he wanted anything. He had not wanted anything. His great head was sunk on his chest; his beard—she had noticed his beard more than anything, the gray bristle, sturdy, almost alive.

"Honey, you don't want that old chair in here. Now, you mustn't grieve," Mrs. Crawford had said this afternoon after the funeral, and after the people who understood had gone.

She was perspiring, for the chair was heavy to carry, but she would not allow Mrs. Crawford to notice the perspiration. "I'm not grieving." She looked straight into Mrs. Crawford's squinched eyes, and she spoke clearly. "My father is nearer to me now than any time since I've been home. I just want the chair in here." Her voice was low and beautiful, she knew, as if the beauty of her father's life had entered her own voice; and she was saying the things her father had always said about death. "He's a part of time, now. Don't you understand that?" Mrs. Crawford did not understand, even though she nodded her mouse-brown head.

In the alcove, where Mamma's great empire sofa with its scarlet velvet cover stood, between the sofa and the wall, was the box. In the box was the doll. It was not fair to think about the doll until all of the street, both sides, the old and the new, was asleep. It was cheating to think about the doll now. But it hadn't been cheating, not really cheating, when she had placed the doll in the box in the corner by the empire sofa the moment she had driven the last person—Mrs. Crawford was the last of course—from the house. She had thought about the doll, without naming her, as she washed the clothes, but she had not felt guilty then. Only now, she must not think about the doll; she must not feel guilty.

For the last two days, more than loss, or grief, or sadness, more than anything which Mrs. Crawford and even the Herricks would expect her to feel, or herself, for that matter, if anyone had told her a week ago that her father would be dead on the fifteenth of May, she had felt clearness. It was hard to fix a word for a feeling. *Clearness*, or *cleanness*, perhaps, and yet they were no more right than *emptiness*. It was exhilarating really to sit in the green chair and to search for the words, while she waited for the Crawford lights to make her own home, her very own home now, the only brightness in the block.

She must keep the emptiness, or clearness, or cleanness. She must not lose the delicate and beautiful balance of the cleaned closet, the cleared window, the empty drawer. It was like being in school again. She would have laughed aloud if she had not covered her mouth with her handkerchief. It was like being in school again, only it was the opposite of school where she wanted to remember every single fact. She must keep the emptiness as she had once kept *learning* in preparation for an examination. She must not think about Dolly. She must not think about the doll.

She held her breath and counted until the clearness returned.

The straight porch chair looked strange, perhaps, sitting, or perhaps it was standing beneath her. The chair had no place in the room, like her father. The room was Mamma's, even though Mamma's breath had not touched the smooth burnished brass and mahogany for three years, almost four, come next Thanksgiving.

She wished that she had stayed at home after Mamma's death, but Pappa had insisted that she go back with Lewis. The two months every summer were not enough to count for a visit. And Lewis had always been with her, scowling at her, or teasing her, always teasing her, and speaking righteously to her, reading his books, oceans and waves of pages of history, every word of which he would remember to take back to Columbia and his little scholars with their glasses and their accents, and complaining of the heat, and refusing to be really nice to her friends, her dearest friends which she had had for ever, until finally, with his scowling, she had stopped trying to see her friends, not much anyhow she saw them, and there were only the breakfasts with Pappa on the side porch, happy laughing breakfasts because Lewis was sleeping on his stomach upstairs—he had worked late—his mouth open, his hair thin and rumpled, the bald spot showing oh so clearly—and she was happy.

Tomorrow there would be another letter from Lewis, pretending great concern. She would not read it. She would put it in the jardiniere which Pappa always used for a wastebasket. She would write a little note, as usual, and she would place it out front, and all day and the next day and the next she could think about her thread of letters slowly, slowly going clear to New York without telling Lewis anything. She would say, "Pappa"—no, Lewis would tease her for calling him Pappa—she would say, "Father's condition is about the same. Hope everything is all right with you. I'll call if I need you." And

64

she would keep writing the letters until Lewis' school was out, and by then even stupid Lewis would understand that she had left him. Lewis would not understand, but Pappa would understand. He had known right from the first how things stood.

She had told Pappa that second summer that Lewis was evil, and Pappa had put his arm around her and said, "You won't want to tell your mother, will you?" and of course she wouldn't tell Mamma, who was stupid and thought Lewis perfectly charming. And she kept going back to New York with Lewis, even after Mamma was dead and there was no reason to go or to keep the secret. She wished she had stayed with Pappa. But even the wishing was not sad; it was timeless; she was tired; a person needed strength to wish; and Pappa had understood. It was strange the way the past sometimes refused to stand still and be counted.

She allowed her eyes to move to the empire sofa and down to the floor where she had placed the box as carefully as if Mrs. Crawford were still in the house. The box had once held a half bushel of apples, and she was very lucky to find the lovely smooth board which just fitted its top. She would have liked to fix up the box, prettily, an old Pennsylvania Dutch design such as they had in the magazines: hearts and flowers, or trailing leaves. The box would be quite handsome—it was clever the way she used the word *handsome*; words were dangerous and exciting. Anyone else who wasn't very careful would have said *pretty*, even if she were just thinking to herself, and the word *pretty* would have recalled the smile of the doll. The box would be quite handsome if it were green, say, with flowers, and yellow satin, quilted, for the lining. She would have fixed it prettily, too, if there had been time; but there wasn't time and this was good. It was a moment of great consciousness and of great maturity.

She did not even jump when the knock came at the door. She might very well have been expecting the knock. She was stiff from having sat in the green chair, but the word *afraid* did not say itself into her mind. There was no room for *afraid* in emptiness.

She turned on the porch light and looked through the beveled glass which made Mrs. Crawford quite laughable-looking in her foolish bathrobe—no one in her right mind would have called it a negligee—with her hands clutched together at the neck.

"I saw the light," Mrs. Crawford said, "and I was thinking about you so much . . ." Mrs. Crawford seemed almost embarrassed.

"That's very sweet of you, Mrs. Crawford."

"Are you all right, honey? You sure you don't want me to come over and stay with you? Walter can listen for the children, and I'd just be more than glad."

"I'm perfectly all right, Mrs. Crawford," she said through the slit of the opened door.

"It's awfully late."

"I'm not sleepy, that's all." She put her hand up to her own throat. She wondered if the blinds on the windows which faced the porch were really closed. "I'm reading. It's all quite pleasant, and peaceful, even." She opened the door wider, holding her mind's breath so that she could not catch the honeysuckle.

"If you're sure," Mrs. Crawford said. "I do wish your husband could have been here."

"You aren't to worry one minute." She shook her head and lowered her eyes. "You're too good; you're much too good."

"I . . . I hope you sleep well," Mrs. Crawford said.

"You go right home and get in bed yourself. And you do understand how I feel, don't you?" And in spite of herself, she said, "Tell me you do understand. Tell me."

"Yes, yes." Mrs. Crawford clenched her hands even more tightly at the neck of her robe.

"You promise?"

"I promise," Mrs. Crawford said, and she looked small and troubled enough to be kissed goodnight.

"Goodnight, dear."

"Goodnight," Mrs. Crawford whispered.

She left the door open and ran to the living room before Mrs. Crawford had reached the second wave of the terrace. But the blinds were tight against the windows.

"Goodnight," she called across the street to Mrs. Crawford.

"Goodnight," Mrs. Crawford said.

Dolly

She stood at the opened door, holding the emptiness balanced within her until Mrs. Crawford closed her own door. She waited, in the midst of the clearness, until Mrs. Crawford turned off all her lights. She waited for longer than necessary perhaps, but she wanted to be sure that the house in which the Crawfords lived and made love and bore children was quite, quite dark.

She made herself walk slowly back into the living room. She looked at the box in the corner, but she did not move toward it. It was like Christmas and wanting to put Pappa's presents under the tree, the slippers or the scarf she had knitted herself, but waiting until the very last minute so the gifts would be fresher for Christmas morning.

The clothes were dry, remarkably so, but she did not move them from the towel. She leaned over the towel, the heat from the grate moving the tie at her bosom, and wound the mantel clock in its glass case with its visible pendulum and spring.

Perhaps Lewis would die tonight. Perhaps he would die as she wound the coil of the spring as tight as a noose. And his death would be loud and harsh and crying, not like Pappa's peaceful slipping away. And they would not find him for a long time perhaps. The people at the university would assume he was ill. If she were at home, she could call and tell his office that he was ill, or had decided on a vacation, and they would think it strange, because they would not know Lewis was dead.

She ran her ring finger and her thumb inside the doll's sweater. She had meant to iron the clothes, but they looked very nice as they were, fitting, really, and the ironing board was in the big pantry off the kitchen, and she had waited much too long already. But before she took the box she moved her finger; and the arms of the sweater came together, almost as if the sweater were applauding.

"Dolly, Dolly," she said.

Once she had been named Josephine, and once Marie, and again Louise, and Katherine, and Vesta, and Dorothy, and Cynthia.

"Dolly," she said.

She held the doll away from her, and the smile on the doll's face was her own. She twirled with the doll; the skirt of her neat black dress twirled about her.

67

It was not cheating to think about Dolly now. It was not cheating. She could sing to Dolly. She could think of anything she wanted to think of. She could dance with Dolly until she fell to the floor beside the towel.

She dressed the doll quickly: the pants, the slip, the organdy dress, the sweater. She smoothed her hands three times over the doll's hair. Then she placed the bonnet on the head; she tied the ribbons of the bonnet carefully so that the sides of the bow were equal.

She cradled the doll in her arm as she walked back to the kitchen and got the hammer and the fourteen nails which she had laid out the day Pappa died. She placed the nails in the tiny pocket over her left breast. She held the hammer behind her until she was again in the living room.

She kissed Dolly once on her smiling lips.

She wrapped Dolly in the towel; she placed her in the box; she closed her own eyes as she fitted the smooth top onto the box.

At first she tried to nail quietly, but it did not matter. The nails lowered themselves, almost, into the rough pine board. Five strokes, and then five strokes, and five strokes again. She removed the nails, one at a time, from her breast. She worked easily. She was surprised when the last nail was gone.

She held the box in both hands, gently, so that there could be no movement. She did not look in the mirror. She was beautiful, she knew, without looking. She did not close the front door behind her. The Crawfords' house was black. She did not mind the noise of her feet on the stepping stones which led back to the garage, or the sound of the motor's coughing.

Pappa's car handled well; it turned into the cemetery quietly. She took her gloves from the compartment even before she turned off the ignition key. She left the box in the car while she dug. It was cool in the cemetery. No other man or woman moved in the coolness. It was too late for lovers, and old Mr. Durham, the caretaker, had long ago gone to bed.

The earth was moist and easy to handle. The flowers all about her were full of wet fragrance. Beside her stood the stone. It would be nice, she thought, if Dolly's name were on the stone, but she did not break the rhythm of her digging.

When she had completed the hole, elbow deep, she brushed her hands together and the dirt scattered over the flowers, like rain. She placed her gloves on the floor of the car and slid the box to the edge of the seat. She lifted it, gently again, and placed it, gently, in the earth. It took only a minute or two to cover the box and replace the flowers.

When she stopped the car in front of her house, she did not even look over to see if Mrs. Crawford were up again.

Concerning, I Suppose, My Father

MOTHER stood inside the living room door. She yawned as she fitted a cigarette into the holder I had sent her from Vietnam. Her face was creased with sleep, but she did not look old. I pushed the telephone away and smiled at my mother.

"It was that damn Hattie, wasn't it?" Mother said.

"I'm sorry the telephone woke you."

"Mamma's dying again, I suppose. Haven't you been to bed yet?"

"I couldn't sleep. I was reading. It doesn't matter."

"It's not as if we hadn't spent the whole afternoon with them." Mother pulled her robe together and came on into the room. "Honestly!"

"We shouldn't have taken them for a drive, that's the trouble. Grandmother thinks she's not at home; she wants to be taken home. It isn't Aunt Hattie." I spoke rather quickly, hoping my mother would not want to pursue the subject.

But she sat on the low chair beside the coffee table. "Dear Lord, it's always something," she said. The lilacs on the table had begun to wilt. I started to mention the lilacs. But my mother said, "They wouldn't even be satisfied if we moved into that pigpen with them, and held their hands, and took them to the bathroom."

"It's a big house. Aunt Hattie has a lot to do. It's natural for her to be wrought up."

"Hattie *loves* being a martyr—I've told you a thousand times. She loves the filth—nice visible signs of her suffering. You can't tell me anything about my family."

"I thought we weren't going to talk about them any more, Mother."

"You're angry now."

"All right. Helen. Helen, it is."

Suddenly my mother laughed. "You're really a Christian saint, Charlie."

"Now, you're making fun of me."

"No I'm not, really I'm not. You're fine. I was just thinking how funny it all is. It's a funny inheritance for you—home from the wars, with a funny inheritance."

"I wish you wouldn't talk that way. I don't even know what you mean."

"Oh, Charlie." Mother switched off the bright lamp above her. Even the movements of her body were young. "Pappa was a good man. And your father is a son of a bitch. Poor Charlie. What are you, Charlie?"

"I'm a saint. You like to say that. You like to be considered the wild one, don't you?"

"Don't be cross. It's just so awful for you to worry about them, and you never go any place—with your own kind, I mean, and you . . ."

"They're our family."

"Oh, baby." Mother shook her head. "Mamma and Hattie should be in an institution, you know that. Mamma's a carnal old woman. If you go there tonight she'll talk about Pappa's coming back from the dead, and she'll be vulgar and offensive; and you'll stand there with your big eyes, almost believing her."

"Maybe. Maybe. You never know—about the institution, I mean." The muscles in the back of my neck hurt. I wanted to rub my neck, but I didn't.

Mother blew smoke toward the fireplace where there was no fire. She watched the smoke until it disappeared. Then she turned quickly, leaning toward me to speak. "You can't be nice to some people, but it's wonderful how loyal you are. I *am* grateful."

"I'm not particularly loyal." I stood up and took the car keys out of my pocket. "What I mean is . . ."

"What do you mean?"

"I don't mean anything, I guess." Mother watched me carefully. "I don't even know what I was going to say."

"We're friends, aren't we?" Mother crossed her legs under the silk of her long gown and smiled at me. "And you'll be glad I sent your father packing. In a while you'll be very glad."

"I don't want to go see Grandmother and Aunt Hattie, you know that."

"Of course I know it. Drive carefully. You will drive carefully, won't you? There's probably fog."

"Don't wait up for me, Helen."

"I'll go right to bed and curse you until I go to sleep." Mother lifted her arms. "Kiss your old mother goodnight."

I let the top of my car down and circled the drive. I looked back at our house. "It is a monument to my parents' divorce," I thought. I had gone to the wars a small-town boy—we lived near Grandmother; I had returned a country gentleman. It was a wonderful house. I had not missed my father. I had not even asked myself why I accepted his absence so easily. If I had asked I suppose I would have said that every world after war is a new world. Still, as I looked at the house I wished, suddenly, that my father could see it. I thought about writing him and asking him down to see what his money had accomplished. I thought about laughing at the thought. I tried to imagine how Helen's face would look if my father should appear. But I did not think about him for long.

It was a pleasant drive into town; the fog was not enough to worry over; I didn't think about anything. I turned on the radio and heard a disc jockey talk about seat covers, and turned the radio off when the music began. There was only the sound of the motor; the white line in the middle of the road moved always a little ahead. I suppose I met five cars; their eyes shone like bright stains, then dimmed. Once, just before the Webster bridge, I felt very close to the eyes of the other driver. The eyes existed alone, for their own sake, and my lights existed alone, outside of myself; the road was a red line on a map, and then, even the eyes did not exist. I caught sight of a part of a tree, new leaves branching over the road, and the face of a house; there was the white line in the center of the road; and, suddenly, the sky was pink ahead of me. I had moved twelve miles through space and I was cold. I stopped at an all-night lunch wagon and bought a package of cigarettes. I put the top of the car up, and I didn't think about anything.

I pulled the bell three times, and waited, and pulled it again. I could see the light through the paneled glass door of the vestibule, even though Aunt Hattie had stretched a Spanish shawl across the glass. Daylight hurt Grandmother's eyes, she said. Upstairs one of Aunt Hattie's roomers coughed. "I'm not taking Helen's money," she always said. "Helen's rejected us. Helen can't stand suffering."

Aunt Hattie pushed back the shawl and nodded to me. "Just as soon as I can get these crazy bolts undone," she called.

I waited while she clawed at the door. "Charlie, Charlie," she said. She swung the door wide and put her arms up to my neck. For a minute she pressed her head hard against my chest. Her thin shoulders shook.

"Hattie, who is it?" Grandmother called.

She lifted her head. She was crying, but her voice was as bright as a child's. "It's Charlie, Mumsey. Charlie's come to see us."

"What's Charlie doing here?"

"He left his jacket this afternoon." Aunt Hattie pushed her fists against her eyes. "Humor her, Charlie. Promise me, promise me."

"Of course."

Aunt Hattie had stopped crying. "Helen's not with you, is she?"

"She has one of those sick headaches."

"I bet. She doesn't think I handle Mother right, does she. She thinks I'm doing wrong. Tell me the truth, before God."

"It doesn't matter."

"Charlie, sometimes I don't think I can stand it. I really don't, seeing poor little Mamma this way. I've been working with her ever since you left. And Helen, it's a hard thing to say, but she doesn't love Mamma. She doesn't love any of us." Aunt Hattie's face worked convulsively.

"Hattie, what are you doing in the hall?"

"I'm just getting Charlie's jacket, Mumsey. Just a minute and we'll be right with you."

Grandmother sat on the edge of the love seat by the front window. The neck of her flannel gown was torn almost to the waist. The room was hot; it smelled of salve and soiled clothes. "Thank the Lord you're here," Grandmother said. "I'm so grateful for you to come and get me out of this awful place."

"What's the matter with my girl?" I kissed her on the forehead.

"Did I tell you your grandfather was back?"

"Yes, you told me."

"When did I tell you?"

Aunt Hattie leaned against the hospital bed which stood where the grand piano used to be. She held a pillow in her arms. She moved her mouth, but I could not understand what she was saying.

"This afternoon you told me—when Helen and I were here."

Aunt Hattie ran around the bed and over to Grandmother. She took one of the safety pins from the towel at her waist. "Goodness sakes, my girl's exposing herself. We weren't expecting Charlie, were we? And awful old Hattie just cut up the gown so Mamma wouldn't get too hot." Aunt Hattie giggled. "You told Charlie about Pappa, in this very room you told him. We're home, Mumsey. And Charlie was as surprised as we were to see Pappa back."

"You wouldn't think a deacon in the church would act like he does, would you?" Grandmother pressed her lips together and nodded. "Fornicating with all the roomers. It's a bad thing. I'd rather see Garvin or Helen come back from the grave. Garvin was a good boy." Grandmother looked up at the picture of Uncle Garvin which hung over the bed. A fly swatter, stuck behind the picture, made its shadow against the wall. "War's pretty bad, but he was a hero, all right. He died for his country."

"Mamma, it's mighty late. Wouldn't you like to go to beddy-bye now that we've seen Charlie?"

"You never tell us anything about your war," Grandmother said. "At least you didn't die, like your mother did. But you're a hero, too. And you're too fine a boy to smoke. I wish you'd never taken it up. You don't look good." Grandmother laughed and placed her hand over her mouth. "Excuse me for not having my teeth in. I mean you don't look like you felt good."

"You aren't to fuss at Charlie," Aunt Hattie said. "He's come to be with us for a little while. And you want your Hattie girl to get some sleep, don't you? It's time we were all getting some sleep."

"It's not time to go to bed yet, Hattie. You're impolite. I want to talk to Charlie. Like we used to when he came to stay with us in the summers. You remember, Charlie? Your daddy used to take your mother gallivanting. Why, you used to be no bigger than my arm. Say something, Charlie."

"We had good times, didn't we?" I said.

Aunt Hattie closed her eyes and ran the back of her hand over her forehead. "It's late, Mamma."

"Well, go to bed, if you're sleepy. I'm not going to bed in this strange house. Sit down, Charlie, for heaven's sake, sit down."

Aunt Hattie began to cry softly. "If you don't get in your bed, I'll lose my mind."

"Hattie!"

"It's time for sweet dreams. Charlie will curl up on the love seat, and I'll

74

just stretch out on the floor right beside your little bed. Mamma, you're not listening to me. Oh, Charlie, it's this way all the time. I never get any sleep. I think she'll drive me crazy." Aunt Hattie dried her eyes with the hem of her towel.

"Charlie, do you remember when you were no bigger than my arm? There were a lot of us then, weren't there? Poor Helen. She went so peacefully. I hope I go like that."

"Look, Grandmother. It's awfully late. You must get in bed."

"Mumsey, baby."

"I'm not going to bed in this house." Grandmother started to stand, then fell back against the cushions.

"This is your house." I spoke loudly. "There's your highboy, and the Rossetti picture, and the Ming vase. And here's that snapshot I sent you from Vietnam. Nobody else has that picture of me. I sent it to you from Vietnam."

"Isn't that strange?" Grandmother said. "It's strange that these people should have a fine young man that looks so much like you."

"There's Uncle Garv's picture. You were just talking about him."

"Poor Garvin. I wonder why God took him. But that's an awful thing to say. A mother saying that! I ought to be ashamed. Help me up, Charlie."

I led her to the bed. "Up we go."

"That's a Mumsey girl. Sweet, sweet sleep."

"No, Charlie. Hold my cane."

She reached under the worn white blanket at the foot of the bed and took out a pink chiffon scarf. She placed the scarf on her head, and Aunt Hattie began to cry. "Now, we'll walk a little." She placed a crocheted antimacassar on top of the scarf. "Back to the bed." She took the white blanket and held it in her arms. She was perspiring. "No, I'm ready. You don't need to help me any more, Charlie."

"Mumsey, Mumsey. Let's take off our clothes." Aunt Hattie patted Grandmother's hands. "Sometimes when people are too hot they get sick at their stomachs and vomit. You don't want to vomit, do you? That's true, isn't it, Charlie? People do get too hot and vomit."

"It's true."

Aunt Hattie tugged gently at the blanket. "Give the cover to Hattie, Mumsey. It's almost summer."

"Charlie, you remember Jim Becks." Grandmother did not let go of the blanket.

"He was before my time." I sat on the corset chair and lit another cigarette. "I knew his grandson."

"You knew Jim, too. He was in the height of your time, but I never hear from him any more. What's happened to him? He was sort of sweet on me." She did not bother to cover her mouth, although she laughed for a full minute. "What's happened to Jim?"

"He's gone," Hattie said.

"Where?"

"Away, Mumsey. Now, let's give Hattie the cover."

"You mean he's dead?"

"Yes, he's dead," I said, even though Aunt Hattie frowned at me.

"Well, I declare." Grandmother shook her head. "The saddest thing in the world is for children to come back to a house and try to make a home of it."

"You have to do it," I said. It was hard to think in the hot room. "You have to keep on living."

"Yes, the preacher was here the other day and looked at your grandfather's books. He said, 'My, what fine books.'" Hattie laid her head on the pillow. Grandmother winked at me. She whispered, "But I didn't tell the preacher what an old cockster your grandfather has turned out to be."

"The preacher was here, in this house. He looked at those books. That proves you are at home."

"Now, Charlie, you know I'm not home."

"What are the books doing there on the shelves, then?"

"Your grandfather's books? I don't know." She was angry. "Somebody must have brought them this afternoon. You gather them right up. We'll take them with us."

"We'll leave the books, but I'm going to take you out in the car," I said. "Right now. Aunt Hattie. Aunt Hattie, are you asleep?"

Aunt Hattie jumped; she cried out. She stood by the bed trembling. Upstairs the roomer coughed. "If she doesn't stop that infernal hacking, I'll kill myself."

"Aunt Hattie, you called me to come here. We're going out now, all of us, in the car."

76

"It's too late, Charlie," Aunt Hattie said. "Don't look at me like that, Charlie. It's all right with me, but I wouldn't want Mother to catch her death of cold. But I suppose it's all right, all right; I tell you, I'll just fix us some coffee—it will do us all good before we take our little trip." Hattie pushed open the sliding doors which once led to the dining room. "It's a mess in here, but there wasn't any place else to store Mamma's good things, and you wouldn't want to trust roomers."

"Aunt Hattie, please. Really."

"Now, don't you fret, Charlie. I won't be a minute, and we'll feel so much better for a little stimulant." She closed the doors after her.

Grandmother reached out to catch the foot of the bed, but I did not move to help her. The blanket dropped to the floor. "Dizzy for a minute," she said. "Let's get out of here before that slut comes back."

"Who?"

"The woman that owns this house."

"That was Aunt Hattie."

"Hattie is a good girl. Everybody loves Hattie. But, dear Lord, how my neck hurts."

"You need to have a good night's rest. Won't you go to bed?"

"I'll just wait, thank you, until we leave this old woman's house."

Grandmother stood beside the bed and told me of Grandfather and the roomers, and of Uncle Garvin, and of Jim Becks. "Yes, yes, of course," I kept saying.

Finally, Aunt Hattie knocked at the sliding doors. She carried a heavy silver tray which held three julep cups of milk. She laughed loudly. "I was afraid the coffee would keep us awake." She had changed into the blue suit which she had bought for my high school graduation; she had not combed her hair, but her lips and cheeks were scarlet. I tried not to look at her.

"Let's have a milk race," she said. "There's nothing like milk, is there? Drink up the milk, and we'll be ready, my precious."

Grandmother pushed the cup away. "Your little boy that lives across the street is mighty cute, Charlie."

"I don't have any little boy. Let's go, please."

"It's your bastard, then."

Aunt Hattie giggled. "How you talk, Mumsey, shame on you. Honestly, she talks about that little boy all the time. She says it looks exactly like you."

"Are you ready?"

"No more Mister Milk, Mumsey?"

"I'll carry you to the car."

"You'll do no such thing. You'll hurt your back. Just give me my cane."

"'Tum on. Let Hattie take one arm, and our Charlie boy will take the other. That's a girl. We're going home, now."

"To our real home?"

"Yes, to our real, real home."

"You bring the blanket, Charlie," Grandmother said.

"No, we don't need it."

"Hattie will bring the blanket. Here's a pillow for Charlie. Mumsey, you carry this." She handed her mother the dirty crocheted scarf from the vestibule table. "Yes, yes, yes, Mother. Yes, yes, yes," she said until we were in the car. "Don't start yet, Charlie. Not quite, not quite." She settled the pillow behind Grandmother's back and wrapped the blanket around her legs. "We don't want our girl to catch the sniffles. All de windows up, all de windows up." She sang as she enveloped her mother. "Could you turn on the heater, Charlie? And we don't want any drafts—your window."

I turned on the heater. I rolled up the window. "But it's warm out," I said.

"Now, we're ready. Unh unh, isn't this fun?" Aunt Hattie's voice broke. She buried her head against Grandmother's shoulder for a moment. "Charlie certainly knows the way. God will take care of us, and Charlie will drive carefully."

"You can't miss with that combination." I tried to laugh.

Grandmother slapped at my wrist. "That's no way to talk. It's sacrilegious." I closed my eyes for a second, but it didn't matter. The streets were empty.

I drove out Tenth to the Newton Pike and over to the Clay's Ferry road and back to Walnut. Grandmother seemed to sleep. "We're about there, aren't we, Aunt Hattie?"

She patted Grandmother's cheek. "Did you hear what Charlie said? He thinks we're almost home. Look out, Charlie, you turn here."

I drove the length of Sycamore.

"We always used to pass the church when we were coming home, didn't we, Mumsey? When we'd been to lovely parties. Wake up, sweetheart, and enjoy your nice ride."

I turned into a service station and swung the car around. Behind the glass of the station a young boy lifted his head from his arms. I lowered the window. "Sorry," I called.

"The draft, Charlie. Careful, careful."

"I'm tired," Grandmother said. "I'm so tired I'm about to die."

"Won't it be good to get in our good comfy beds, though?"

"Yes, it will be good," I said.

Grandmother began to sing. "Oh, that will be glory for me."

Aunt Hattie joined the song. "Sing, Charlie," she said, and I hummed along with them.

"That was your father's favorite song," Grandmother said. "My husband, I mean. Nobody knows anything about your father."

"Silly Mamma." Aunt Hattie kissed Grandmother's ear. "Were you singing about heaven or bed?"

"Heaven."

My mind recorded their words. I tried to think of what they said, but I couldn't.

"It was ugly of me to say *bed*. I'm tired, too. But God will take care of us."

"Yes, honey, I hope and pray he will."

"I love you," Hattie said.

"I'm not much good."

"Yes, you are, don't you talk that way. Your prayers have done a lot for me. I don't know what I'd have done without them."

"You're a good child, Helen."

"Hattie. Hattie. I'm Hattie, Mamma."

"There's the church," I said, "and the parsonage. Which way do we turn now?"

"Charlie doesn't even know the way; isn't that a sight?"

"He doesn't do so bad," Grandmother said.

"There's Thompson's Grocery. We'll soon be home. And will I ever be glad!" Aunt Hattie sobbed, then laughed. "Mamma, Mamma. The lights of home. They're waiting for us. Thank God, I say it reverently."

79

"Thank God," Grandmother said. "I hope your daddy's there."

"He will be." Hattie started unwrapping Grandmother even before I had pulled to the curb. "Daddy's back there singing and playing. I just know he is."

"Playing with who?"

"With little cards." Aunt Hattie laughed.

"Shame on you, Hattie. He never would allow cards in the house and you know it."

"I was only teasing."

After I had carried Grandmother to the porch, after Aunt Hattie had found her key, after we had closed the door behind us, we stood in the vestibule for a minute without speaking, as if we had just come home from a party.

"How good it is to be here!" Grandmother sighed. "I'm sure Charlie's hungry. You want a bite to eat, don't you?"

"Thank you, I've eaten."

"What did you eat?"

"I can't remember, but it was a fine meal. I'm full as I can be. Now you two get to bed and have a good night's rest."

"You're sure you don't want anything to eat?"

"I'm sure. I hope you sleep well."

"The same to you, honey." Grandmother kissed me. "Goodnight."

Aunt Hattie followed me out on the porch. "I may have to call you again. Sometimes she gets almost violent."

"It's all right. I don't mind. I hope you can rest."

"Thank you, sweetheart. Goodnight. You can thank Helen for letting us borrow you." Aunt Hattie kissed me.

"Goodnight," I said.

I lowered the windows in the car and sat for a minute before I started the engine. I wondered if my mother were asleep. I thought about going down on First Street to see Gladys, or Evelyn, or Sylvia. Most of them knew my father. They seemed to like to talk about him. But it was very late, and I was tired anyhow, so I went home that night.

The Man Who Looked Young

H E WAS forty-two years old. He would not feign modesty. He looked as if he were twenty-four or twenty-five. Regularly, friends, acquaintances, said their surprise at his age. He was a kind of parlor game in Darien, Connecticut, and Athens, Ohio. "How old do you guess Wes Hopkins is?" people asked each other. The highest age reported was twenty-seven. He was pleased at how many people had told him about their guessing games. Only a few weeks ago a new man at the Ohio State Liquor Store asked for his I.D. card. When Wes took out his driver's license from the billfold Agnes had given him for his birthday, the man said, "My God, kid. Did you steal this?" But the man, shaking his head, found the bottles he had signed for. The man looked old. He had not shaved well under his nose or on the right side of his chin. He said, "God damn it, I'm forty-one."

"Have a good day," Wes said. He did not approve of people who said, "Have a good day." He always meant to have any kind of a day he damn well pleased. But sometimes situations demanded an innocuous valedictory.

When Dot and he were in New Zealand Wes started saying, "Good on you." He liked the words. He said, "Good on you" at every conceivable occasion. Perhaps he sounded affected. He did not like to sound affected. Back in the states, after a series of disapproving stares from clerks, friends, acquaintances, he stopped saying "Good on you." He missed the words. He liked flamboyant farewells, even casual ones. He would have liked to have said, "Fare thee well," or "God go with you," to the wrinkled flabby squinting people he was always leaving. He liked the feel of his own youth and grace, blessing somebody.

DOT and he had stayed for three months in New Zealand, seeing every blessed sheep of it. Dot adored the place, even more than Austria or Japan. He did not lose patience with her. He almost never lost patience. All of his life he had refrained from losing patience, saving his impatiences for a few large quiet scenes. "I said to her, I said . . ." his mind often recorded. "I said to him . . ." "She was crying softly. She was ugly as sin. I said . . ."

Dot said, "New Zealand is a little Switzerland, a little Ireland, a little England."

Only once did he say, "But we've seen the real Switzerland, and Ireland, and England."

Dot said, "Of course, darling, that's why it's so much fun," while they rushed to a travel agency to cancel another plane home.

"Good on you," he said to Dot as they recircled the north island and the south island, resting comfortably in hotels that were the real Hilton.

H E missed the travel. He missed the comfortable Connecticut existence and Dot's totally endless monies. But he was not ultimately sorry they had separated. The girl in Phoenix was nothing. He would rather have been separated over the girl in Auckland, or the woman in Boulder, or the boy in Honolulu. He could have chosen a dozen better occasions for separation than the girl named Jennifer. Already he could not remember her last name. She was neither more attractive nor better in bed than Dot. She was a crying hedgehog. He did not even have a losing-patience scene to remember with Jennifer.

"You win a few, you lose a few," he told himself often, standing in front of the full-length mirror, smoothing his hands over his thick hair.

Dot's settlement was more than adequate. He was grateful for Dot's warped mind that functioned in her unattractive body. Who else would have arranged such an adequate settlement for a wandering, attractive husband? He did not want to think evil of Dot. If she entered the apartment now he would say, "Good on you, Dot!" The checks from her attorney came on the fifteenth of every month. He had circled the *fifteens* of every page of the leather and gold five-year calendar by his bedside table. The room sported two more-than-adequate twin beds, each with a bedside table. Dot had sent him the calendar for his birthday on Halloween after he was already living in Athens.

For four months Athens, Ohio, had been his home. He was proud of living in Athens. He had chosen chance.

"You've got to get out," Dot said the last night of his Connecticut existence. It was the last of July. She was crying quietly. She was particularly ugly when she cried.

He moved away from her to the vast mahogany secretary that had belonged to her great-great-great grandmother. He smoothed his hands over the wood that was lovelier than flesh. Dot relished his appreciation of her old pieces.

After four months he missed most the elegance of their parlor.

He had taken out the huge atlas they had studied a thousand times together. It was a fine moment. It was fine to hand Dot his gold pen. It was fine to say, "Take this pen." It was exhilarating to say, "Close your eyes." Dot was foolishly obedient. It was fine to say, "Lower this pen on to the map."

When he was young, his sister and he had played with omens. They had lived in Methodist parsonages all over Nebraska and Kansas. "Let's play with the Bible," he often said to Tina. She was a beautiful girl. She was to die of appendicitis, even though dying of appendicitis had gone out of style by the time he was twelve and she was fourteen.

"Let's play with the telephone book," Tina whispered.

"Close your eyes, Tina. Take this crayon. Make a mark."

He riffled the pages of the telephone book. Tina was trembling. "Here. This page."

"You're silly, Wes," Tina said, obediently lowering her crayon.

They called whatever name she marked. "Mr. Kemmerle?" "Mrs. Williams?" "Mr. Keyes?" "Mrs. Thompson?"

"This is The Shadow," he said to the telephone.

Once in April, playing with the Bible, Tina's crayon dropped to a passage that said, "They shall come in the night to slay thee." They giggled together, holding each other.

Tina said, "We shouldn't play with the Bible." She was crying. She cried softly. "Daddy wouldn't like it."

"It's my Bible. He won't know."

"That's true, Wes. I'm sure that's very true."

"The Bible doesn't mean anything."

"You shouldn't say that. You shouldn't be talking that way, Wes."

But the Bible was right.

She was dead in three weeks.

83

D o t closed her eyes. "Quit being silly, Wesley. You're scaring me, Wesley."

The lines on Dot's face were like road maps. Tina's face never knew lines.

"It's a map of the United States. Lower the pen, Dot. Lower the pen." He was excited. It was a fine sexual moment, but he did not touch the woman.

"Wesley, please don't make me."

"Lower." He could have been a villain in a motion picture, a late television show full of fog horns and snarling cats. The house was very quiet. Dot's breathing was the only sound, obliterating the Cloisonné clock on the mantel.

"Open your eyes. Where am I going?"

"Ohio." Saliva formed at the corners of Dot's mouth. She looked like all of the witches in the world.

"Where?"

"Athens, Ohio."

He had chosen chance.

His suitcases were already packed.

"G o o d n i g h t, Dot. Good-bye." He did not kiss her, although she was crying quietly, although she was trying to throw her arms around him.

She babbled. "I won't, I don't want to go through with it. We won't get divorced. I was just upset. That girl, that's all right. It doesn't matter, Wesley. I love you Wesley."

It was pleasant to hear her say, "I love you." She did not like to admit love, or need.

"I need you, Wesley."

"I hate to be a bother. You'll pick up the car at the airport. Somebody can pick up the car, the little car. Good on you, Dot."

Dot called his name until his name was no more a name than the sound of fingernails clawing at a blackboard.

The good-bye had been totally satisfactory.

I t was simpler to adjust to Athens, Ohio, than to get there.

At the airport he told the sleepy girl at the desk, "I'm going west, south. Athens, Ohio."

She had never heard of the place.

84

"West, then." He was sure that Dot would be at the airport in a little while, crying, looking ugly.

"There's a plane for Chicago in twenty minutes."

"Chicago," he said, feeling tall and free. The girl was smiling at him. She was awake now. She ran her tongue over her full lips.

"I'm forty-two years old," he said.

"You're kidding. You're kidding me. That's how old my daddy is."

It was not pleasant to spend a night in O'Hare, but he slept, waiting for a plane to Columbus, waiting for a rented car to Athens, Ohio. He remembered the night as he remembered dreams.

"You can't get there from here," people at desks kept saying.

"It's farther than it is," people said.

HE arrived in Athens, Ohio, at noon. By dusk he had rented a sixth-floor apartment in Lake Edge Manor, a set of buildings on the top of a hill, in sight of no water. But the view was like a birthday card for somebody born in autumn. Ohio, the world, lay pieced, a Ladies' Missionary Society quilt, outside his living room balcony. The balcony was very attractive, large enough for sitting on, or throwing yourself from.

When he was a child they had made a lot of Christmas. Even he and Dot had made a lot of Christmas. For sixteen years they had trimmed a tree, and invited people in, and sung carols. After you are forty, sixteen years does not seem a very large number. Dot played her grandmother's piano poorly. The people who sang "Oh, Come All Ye Faithful" and "Silent Night" were patient. They held notes while Dot fumbled for the keys.

But it was more pleasant to live in a university town than in a bedroom town. Ohio University is larger than Athens, Ohio. The lonely people, remembering other towns, reach out for the stranger. The second night at Lake Edge Manor he ate dinner with the couple next door, two vast people named Reams who had recently spawned vast twins. The meal was rubber noodles and tomato ketchup. He was grateful that Dot was barren. He disliked the Reamses, but they were very kind. The next night he took them to the Walnut Room for dinner. The outing was a mistake. They were painfully poor and appreciative. Perhaps he should have offered to pay for their sitter. But he did not offer. He was embarrassed at their fumbling through drawers and purses to find enough quarters for the girl down the hall. The sitter could not have been thirteen, not so old as Tina. She stood first on one foot, then another, chewing violent gum. She would become a beautiful woman. Already she was a beautiful woman. She was conscious he was watching her. For a moment she stopped chewing and smiled at him.

"Good-bye," he said to the Reamses after they had had a beer together. They were not worth arranging a flamboyant farewell for. Ruby Reams boasted both a mustache and a goatee. She leaned heavily against him when he said his simple "Good-bye." Always she was excessively friendly in the elevator and at the automatic washers in the basement.

A SINGLE man, young enough to be asked for his I.D. card at the State Liquor Store, quickly manages to become an Athenian. He enrolls for the winter quarter as a special student in a course named The Renaissance and Other Contemporaries. He subscribes to a concert series, a lecture series, the Private Appalachian Club, an occasional showing of pornographic movies. He learns to avoid most of the Reamses of the world; he meets a variety of students and young faculty members. He eats all over town, at Bromley, and the Deli, and the Union Bar, and acquaintances' houses. He frequents bars. He meets Zach at a bar. Zach's father is from Darien, in advertising. Zach's father is a long-time acquaintance. Zach's father is a son of a bitch. Young Zach says it is a small world. Zach's father once arranged for Wes Hopkins to attend him and a couple of his buddies on a fishing trip to northern Ontario. The trip was a fiasco. Zach's father was a masterful fisherman. He ridiculed people who did not catch fish. Old Zach's buddies managed a good catch every day for a week.

Dot considered Old Zach totally admirable.

Young Zach groped for a picture of his girl. "Agnes. She's named Agnes. We live together sometimes. I wouldn't want my dad to know." Zach's hand trembled as he pulled the picture from his billfold. His billfold bulged with identifications. The boy was small. He sported a Groucho Marx mustache. He was painfully thin. He wore a gold earring in his left ear.

"She's in dance. She's very cultured."

86

"Wow!" Wesley said, holding the picture close to and then away from his eyes. He needed glasses. Soon he would make an appointment for glasses. Agnes was not attractive. She looked rather like Dot.

Wesley Hopkins courts chance. Wes searches for chance, choosing chance.

He met Agnes on an October Friday, at Memorial Auditorium, after a ballet. Small snow fell outside the door, against the flood lights that made the building look like a building in a dream.

"Thank you," Agnes said. "Thank you very much."

"We're going to the Capital Bar. You'll have a drink with me," he said, pretending even to himself he did not recognize the girl with the thin lips and the long lank hair.

"I shouldn't. I really shouldn't. My boyfriend wouldn't like it. He doesn't like ballet. I told him I was going straight home to study. I shouldn't. I really shouldn't. He's in business administration." She could have been Dot a thousand years ago, or a thousand years from now.

She was a small girl, smaller even than Tina or Dot. Her face was shaped like a lopsided valentine. He liked valentine-faced girls. Her hair hung almost to her waist.

In the bar Agnes asked, "What year are you? I mean, I don't want to sound inquisitive, I'm just interested. People are my hobby."

"I'm out of school. I'm a long time ago. I'm forty-one years old, forty-two in a week."

"I'm older than that. I'm a hundred and eight."

After three drinks they took a taxi to Lake Edge Manor. "I really shouldn't," Agnes kept saying. "I really shouldn't. Zach will be furious." She took a picture of Zach from her wallet. He could not see the boy's face in the dark of the taxi. "Handsome," he said. "Very handsome."

She was a frightened girl but cooperative.

"You are beautiful. You are very beautiful," Agnes said. "I'm on the pill. That's good, isn't it? Isn't that very good?"

Agnes said, "Darling, oh my darling." She said, "Oh my darling, darling."

He said—he could not really remember what he had said. He had probably said, "You'll stay." Whatever he had said was not a question.

"I shouldn't. I really really shouldn't. I have a roommate."

He probably said, "I'm your roommate."

"Oh lovely Wes." She was laughing softly. She laughed and laughed until she was almost crying. It was difficult to remember her name.

She wore a fraternity pin on her grimy blouse. "I won't take it off, the pin. Zach and I are pinned."

He said, "I thought pinning had gone out of style, like dying of appendicitis."

"No, not really, not for us." She talked a great deal about Zach. "You're better than Zach. You're a thousand times better. But I'm in love with Zach. I'm in love with you also. You know that. But you're better."

She was a charming and inventive child.

She stayed for four nights and three days. She did not leave the apartment except to buy him the billfold, at Cornwell's, on Saturday. She refused to go out to eat. She sent him down the hill for noodles and hamburger meat. For three days they ate noodles and meat balls. "I love to cook. I'm very domestic. I'm an earth mother. That's what Zach says. He learned it in a class."

On Monday evening Wes asked, "Does everybody in Athens, Ohio, eat noodles and meat balls three times a day?"

"You don't like my cooking. I'm a good cook. You don't like me." She was crying.

It was an exhilarating good-bye. "Get the hell out of here. Get your ass out of this apartment," he whispered to Agnes.

Agnes cried softly. Nobody in the apartment building could have heard her crying. He had chosen this day. If it were chance that he looked young, he was determined to choose the farewells of his life. "Get your ass out."

THE morning after Agnes went back to her other roommate, Zach visited Lake Edge. The day was cold, twenty degrees, the radio said. Zach wore a pink T-shirt and a skinny hand-knitted scarf. His neck bones pressed through his shirt.

"I don't want you fooling around with Agnes. I just found out. She called me. She was crying."

Wes extended his hand. "Good to see you, Zach."

"I don't want you fooling around with Agnes." The boy stuffed his hands deep into the pockets of his blue jeans.

"I'm through fooling around with Agnes. She's a lousy cook."

"She's good with noodles."

"She left yesterday. Come in. Have a drink. Let's talk about Agnes. Or your father. Let's talk about your father. I'm forty-two years old."

"I know you are. Everybody knows you are. You're older than my daddy." Zach slammed the door so hard that the Coptic cross, one of the few *objets* he had brought from Connecticut, fell from the wall. He did not know why he had chosen to bring the Coptic cross.

THE walls of the men's room in the basement of Ellis Hall bore handsome graffiti, drawings, invitations, quotations, telephone numbers.

"Robin Hood wears panty hose."

"God is a Jew."

"So's your sister."

Wes dialed 592-4156 from the telephone booth at the student center.

"Chance," he said, almost knowing that Zach would answer, almost sure he had seen Zach's telephone number on an identification card in the billfold that held a picture of Agnes. "Choice," he said.

The call was an act of choice, not chance. He was not surprised to hear Zach's ragged voice.

"Zach? It's Wesley. Wes Hopkins."

"I'll be there," Zach said. "Sure. Your place. No hard feelings?"

"I hope so. At seven. We'll have lasagna. I'm up to my armpits in noodles."

Zach laughed a little. "I like lasagna. I'll be there." He slammed down the receiver, hard enough to deafen a man.

But he was a gentle boy. "A man knows what a man wants," Zach kept saying. He was very adept. "Maybe Agnes will come with us sometime."

"I don't want Agnes. No, no, no, Zach." For not any reason he was thinking of Zach's fisherman father.

"No, no, no, no," Zach said after him. "Now, now, now."

Zach left at midnight. "The hands fold," Wes said. He was terribly sleepy. He could not remember when he had had a good night's sleep.

"Sure enough." Zach looked at his wristwatch.

"It's been a good evening. Goodnight, fellow. We'll have it again."

"Goodnight." Zach did not lift his eyes from his watch. He turned to the door, fumbling for the knob.

"Have a good night's rest."

"The same to you."

FIFTEEN minutes later the doorbell rang. Wes was just out of the shower. He was annoyed with the idea of Zach's returning. The boy could become a problem. But not much of a problem. He would say, "Get your ass out of this apartment." He would have a good farewell with Zach, getting the boy and his father told off. Perhaps he would write Zach's father, telling on the boy. He would not write anonymously. He would sign his name in large black letters.

He pressed the buzzer. He said, "Up, up, up. Come on up if you can get up." He spoke sleepily. He did not try to make his voice young and vigorous. Perhaps he sounded like an old man. He rather hoped he was sounding like an old man. Enough of Zach was enough.

It was Dot.

She wore her old black fur-lined raincoat and a plastic hat he had never seen before. She was crying. She lifted her arms to embrace him. They did not kiss. Dot, crying, rubbed her face against his chest, calling his name.

"I couldn't stand it, Wesley," she said against his chest. "I've been driving for two days. In snow, Wesley. It was terrible. I thought I was going crazy, Wesley."

He held his arms stiff against his sides. He had almost forgot to say, "Good on you." He said, "Good on you, Tina. Christmas is coming."

She threw her head back. Her mouth was open. He could see the fillings in her teeth. She looked as if she were gargling. She lowered her arms and turned away from him. The foolish plastic hat fell to the floor.

"I said 'Tina,' didn't I?" He laughed. He was genuinely amused. His laugh was not at all affected.

"I'm Dot." She lowered her head. Her dyed brown hair was wet and matted. There were strands of gray in her hair.

"I know you are. Of course you are." He hoped there was pity in his voice. He hoped the disgust he felt for the thin old woman did not sound in the room. But he was very tired. She would want to be taken to bed, of course.

Old maid that she was, she would still want to be taken to bed. The thought of her body filled him with revulsion, as real as vomit in his throat.

"You've had company." She leaned over, as if to pick up the two glasses. The ice had melted in the glasses, leaving liquid the color of urine.

"Oh, yeah. Young Zach Lyle. He came for dinner. He's a fine young man."

"I knew you'd seen him. Big Zach told me the other day, in the grocery. The boy writes them every week." She turned suddenly. "I wish you'd answered my letters. Do you realize I haven't heard from you, not one word, not in all these months? Not one word. A lot of times I've started to call you. I have your telephone number. I've called information a number of times to get your number. It's been a kind of comfort, calling information." Her eyes were steady. "Talk to me, Wesley."

He tightened the belt of his robe. "We've done all the talk, Dot."

He said, "We've talked enough. Let me take your coat. Sit down, won't you? Let me fix you a drink."

"No. No, thank you. Not anything, thank you." But she was taking off the old raincoat. She wore a harsh green skirt and sweater he had never seen before. Her skin was the color of the liquid in the glasses.

He stood holding the coat for a minute, not knowing what to do with it. "The closet," he said, going to the vestibule, hurrying. Zach had left the scarf Agnes had knitted him for Christmas. Dot's clammy raincoat slipped from the hanger. "Shoot," he said aloud. He did not even own a gun. He hung up the coat again. The lining of the coat was wet, as if Dot had used her thin matted hair for the lining. He could not imagine how the lining could have been wet.

In the kitchen, at the galley counter, he filled himself a water glass of bourbon. "You don't mind, do you?"

"I don't mind." She had moved to the red chair. She lowered herself, bracing herself on the chair arms. She looked like a dilapidated Christmas decoration. He chose the chair opposite her, on the other side of the coffee table. He smoothed the skirt of his robe over his knees.

"I've been worried about you." Her eyes were very steady.

"Glug, glug," he said. The drink was warm. "I'm fulfilled. Bourbon is very fulfilling."

"If only you'd written. I wouldn't have worried if you'd written. You're looking thin. Why haven't you written? Not one word?"

He was not going to argue with her. He honestly did not want to hurt her feelings. He did not want her to start crying. He wanted . . .

He wanted only for her to die. How simple and comfortable it would be if her head slumped, if her body fell from the red chair. "Coronary, a massive coronary," the doctor would say. "Our sympathies," the funeral director would say. For sixteen years he had listened to her questions, and endured her monologues. There was no reason to listen any more.

"I'm almost forty, Wesley. It's hard for a girl to be almost forty, and alone."

He, too, was holding tightly to the arms of his chair, the white chair veined with red. He was sorry she had chosen to call herself "girl."

"Why are you here?" He put his hands around his empty glass.

"I was worried. I've been worrying about you. I need, Wesley. I need you."

He had ordered his life. Dot's appearance was chance. He had not chosen her appearance. He said, "Your coming is an accident. I told you a long time ago, I told you I don't believe in accidents. Ergo, I don't believe you're here." He had learned to say "Ergo" from the art history teacher.

"Wesley, don't talk that way. You're scaring me, Wesley." Her knuckles shone white on the chair arms. "I'm here, Wesley. I've come to take you back home with me, to our home. Can you hear me, Wesley?"

THE little scene could have ended variously.

He said, "We're not quarreling, Dot. You're still my wife."

He could have said, "You'll spend the night. We'll make love. You like for me to make love to you. I suppose what I do best is making love."

"You'll go back to Connecticut. We'll continue the lives we have chosen. You chose first, remember."

He could have said, "Let me show you the apartment. It's really very pleasant. There's room for the two of us. Single beds. But that's all right. Single beds can be pulled together. Remember that time in Florence."

"Here's the kitchen. It's a nice kitchen. The disposal will swallow everything. You can cut up anything and it will swallow. Here's the study. I've enjoyed studying here. I've become very learned about the Renaissance and our contemporaries."

He could have said, "The bathroom. Everything works. The pressure's fine. We can shower and bathe together, or apart. That time in Cairo. You remember that time in Cairo. And then we'll go into the kitchen."

"You're leaving tonight. Right now. You're getting your ass out of this apartment."

"You're staying. You'll like Athens. The people are friendly. They are very kind to strangers."

"Of course we'll go back to Darien. I want to see the old friends. I want to see the Lyles, for instance. Old Zach is a good old camping buddy."

"Here's the balcony. The windows get dirty, but I don't mind washing them. I like to wash them, window spray and paper towels, a whole roll of paper towels. I have a cleaning woman twice a week, but I always do the doors to the living room balcony. Outside the balcony lies all Ohio. You'll sit out here on sunny days. You can sun bathe, naked. We're protected. Your skin will be the color of honey."

Dot would shiver in the cold night, watching all of Ohio. She would be holding her arms together, holding herself together against the Christmas card night.

"It's far down. It makes me dizzy, Wesley."

"I have friends here, young friends. They think I'm their age. They have a lot of names. They will testify for me. They will say anything I tell them to say. I have other friends, too. I'm invited out to dinner a lot. The Reamses. And the head of the English department. People at the concerts and lectures. And my teacher, Professor Alexander. I'm a patron of the arts, Dot. What do you think of that?"

Dot could not weigh over a hundred pounds. It would be a simple matter to stand behind her, pressing against her. She liked that. She would fall from the balcony without difficulty. Her falling would be no more impossible than throwing an empty cigarette package over a bridge into a river. The mark of her body on snow would be no more lasting than a snow angel. He and Tina had made a thousand snow angels, laughing, lying in the snow, spreading their arms and legs, apart and together. "Snow angels," Tina said. "We are snow angels."

"We are snow angels," he said.

Dot lay in the other bed, the bed he never used.

"Good on you," he said over and over, sorry that he had nothing more to say, not caring at all, at all, not giving one good God damn, confessing the ovum of choice and chance, knowing only that youth was an impossible burden.

Diving

TODAY is Monday. I am fond of Mondays, although I have never gone around saying so, not wanting to offend most of the people I know who speak regularly of gloomy Mondays and Monday blues.

I have not realized until recently that I am fond of Mondays because of our son Mark. I am surprised and pleased to recognize my inheritances from the children. Last night I told Anna that I had probably inherited more from Robert and Mark and Charlotte than they have inherited from me.

Anna said, "I've been thinking about Mark, too. But you aren't planning to write a story about him?"

"I want to, Anna. It won't be a sad story." I quoted Mark, "Oh boy, a whole new week. A birthday and a Monday! Remember?"

Anna shrugged. "And Robert and Mark would argue. Markie never would agree that Sunday was the first day of the week." Anna was smiling.

I had forgot. It is a pleasure to remember.

Anna had wanted to have a party for Mark's twelfth birthday, inviting every boy in his room—Miss Hattie's class. Mark said he'd rather not. "Why don't us guys go to Lake Baldwin? We haven't been there in a month of Sundays."

Mark delighted in phrases like a month of Sundays, fine as frog's hair, crooked as a corkscrew. And after he was in bed he always called, "Sleep tight; don't let the bedbugs bite." I could make a litany of Mark's sayings. "Knock, knock, who's there?"

Robert thought Lake Baldwin was a good idea; Charlotte, only four, was not yet old enough to consider any family gathering too barfy for endurance.

I reminded Anna of her saying that, for mothers, every birthday party was more exhausting than any birth.

"I know, I know. I really loathe birthday parties. But you should have something to remember on your twelfth birthday."

"But he wants to go to Lake Baldwin."

"Sure. O.K. Marvelous."

The five of us set out at eleven in the morning. Mark got to choose his place in the car—the window seat up front. Mark had chosen the menu. Anna had fixed lima beans in the hot thermos; four-bean salad, sauerkraut in the cold thermoses; peanut butter and bleu cheese sandwiches; the ice chest held two cartons of Cokes and a chocolate cake that said, "Happy Returns, Mark, Old Man."

We were Protestants conducting a mitzvah.

Anna told me to put the food in the trunk of the car while she rounded up the towels and bathing suits. The telephone rang. It was a wrong number.

We had an old Ford then, tan, which broke down on bridges—only a few bridges, but enough to give itself a reputation. I admired that car. We fitted into it exactly.

We arrived at Lake Baldwin about noon. I had forgot my wristwatch. I was pleased with having forgot.

It was the finest September day I can remember in a life of fine September days. It was a gold day. A few impossibly white clouds postured around in the sky, proving how blue a September day could be. The dogwood leaves had already turned dark pink and mahogany, the sumac burned scarlet; a few poplars and beeches yellowed the edge of the little lake, but most of the trees were green green. We had had a muggy summer, but that day was worth waiting for through months of muggy summer.

We were the only people at the lake. The park had closed officially on Labor Day. There was a small sign, "Swim at your own risk," but the whole place said welcome.

That was one day I did not say, "Be careful," or "Not too far out," or, "Stop that arguing." I cannot remember many such outings.

The bathhouses were two big rooms made of logs, open to the blue sky, with high window squares to be looked through only if you stood on a bench. "Gee, it's like a fort," Mark said. "I forgot it was like a fort."

The boys were into their trunks in seconds. They were already in the water before I got my trousers off. Standing on the bench, I watched the boys through one of the square portholes.

It is a pleasure for a man to watch his sons.

Charlotte appeared at the door. She wore the ruffled pants. "Mamma is stuck."

"Charlotte," Anna called from her fort.

"She's in here, in the men's room." Back then it was funny for Charlotte to be in the men's room.

"Well, bring her in here and help me with this darned zipper."

In the ladies' room I swung Charlotte to my shoulders. Anna and I kissed. Charlotte patted our heads.

Anna said, only half mocking, "Charlotte is an angel, blessing her parents."

Charlotte said, "Schawl-ut is a angel, angel, angel." She waved her arms over her head. "Schawl-ut is a angel, skippety mum per lou."

"You know what the last one in is," the boys called as they had always called. They stood on the stationary platform in the middle of the swimming area. Each held to the ladder of the high diving board.

"How's the water?" we asked as we had always asked.

"The water's fine."

Charlotte ran screaming into two inches of water, and out, and in again.

"Let's see a dive," Anna called.

Robert said, "You go first, Mark. It's your birthday."

Mark said, "Maybe I'll do it right this time, but you go first. You show me."

Oh, I am poorly put together. I was always touched when the boys were gentle with each other. I didn't look at Anna.

Robert dived, not a spectacular dive, but an adequate one. We applauded. Mark said, "That was pretty neat. Better'n all right."

Robert did everything better than all right: tennis, carpentry, his school work. Only on rare occasions was he struck with a passion—his leaf collection won first prize at the state fair in Louisville; when he was fourteen his history of Graham County, written because he wanted to write it, was published as a pamphlet by the state historical society. Robert moved gracefully through being young.

Mark's enthusiasms embraced the world. He excelled in enthusiasm. He was never so efficient as Robert, but he did everything with a passion. He worked hard and with joy; I can't remember his ever expressing disappointment over any failure. He was particularly poor at diving. We watched Mark dive five or six times, fall, rather, to belly flop, to try again, his stomach as red as a lobster. "Was that better? Was that a little better? Here I go again. Watch. Watch now."

"O.K. Let's see you," Anna called.

Charlotte stopped being a sandpiper to look at Mark.

The boy stood on his toes, raised his hands, smiled at us, breathed deeply, and soared.

Mark floated in the air, gold colored against the blue, against green, knifing into the water, his body as straight as an exclamation point.

I held my breath as if I, too, had flown, as if I were under water, pushing toward the sun.

Mark appeared from far out in the water, beyond the buoys that marked the swimming area. He began to swim, clumsily, back to the platform.

Charlotte squealed.

Robert said, "Gol-lee."

Anna held her hands over her mouth. There were tears in her eyes. "My. Lovely," Anna said against her hands.

Mark, awkward, climbed onto the platform. Robert slapped him on the back. We shouted our congratulations. Charlotte sang, "Markie is a bir-ud, skiptum skiptum dee."

"I did it, didn't I?" Mark was shivering.

"Like the Olympics," Anna called.

Mark was embarrassed. "You all shut up."

That day was one of those rare days when Time shows off, when it performs all the tricks it is capable of. It lingered. We swam, we lay in the sun. Charlotte slept. "We should eat, shouldn't we?" Anna and I asked each other every once in a while. The sun stood high in the sky.

"They're having such fun."

Again and again Mark dived. He was never to move so exquisitely as he had moved that long floating minute; but Mark had learned to dive.

Time had raced.

Robert and Mark stood over us. "I'm hungry," Mark said. "My stomach's stuck to my backbone."

"Yeah. When are we going to eat?"

As I walked toward the car I realized I had failed to bring the ice chest and thermoses from the kitchen table.

Anna said, "You couldn't have forgot."

"Wow! A birthday dinner without any food."

Mark began to laugh. He rolled in the sand, laughing.

They were not cross with me. We gathered our gear and raced home. We had our picnic on the back porch. It must have been four-thirty or five when we ate.

That day was a good day to happen to a boy on his twelfth birthday: a perfect dive, watched by all of his family.

2.

For almost a year now I have been devoting the weekends to writing. It has been a pleasant experience.

Actually I have been writing for Anna. It was Anna's suggestion that I start—Anna's and Dr. Thorndike's. A couple of years ago I had a little bout of depression, nothing serious, just average middle-aged depression. I'm fine now, but Anna has insisted that I keep at the writing. "You'll have a book before you know it," Anna has kept saying. "It's a way to save time, Arch. Really *save* time."

I have looked forward to the evenings of the days when I have written. Anna has read the stuff aloud to me, the little essays, the stories my grand-father used to tell me, the memoirs—whatever it is I'm writing. At some few passages she has almost cried. Sometimes she has laughed. "You're really saving time, Arch."

It has been pleasant to hear Anna read. I have lain on the couch in the den, my arms under my head, and studied the ceiling. I have smiled at the ceiling. Anna has a lovely voice. My words sound good in Anna's voice.

Yesterday, Saturday, was Anna's morning at the museum. I had just finished writing about Mark's birthday when she came home.

"How did the writing go?" she asked, as she always asks.

"So so. I've written about Mark's twelfth birthday. You can read it now. I'm through for the day. It's been a nice morning."

"We must keep to the schedule," Anna said kissing me. "If you're really through, we'll go shopping. Christmas is a coming."

"He was a fine boy."

"We can start by getting some no-surprises for each other—the books we really want. We never mean it when we say we aren't going to get each other

99

anything. Do we? You're planning to cheat, aren't you? You're planning to get me something marvelous."

I admitted that I planned to cheat.

"I'm glad. I'm glad you don't have a lot of character."

It was a fine day yesterday. The afternoon was warm enough for only a jacket.

We attended, at Anna's insistence, only expensive department stores where most of the customers looked as affluent as the Christmas decorations. We watched the skaters at the Galleria. We had tea and little sandwiches at a tea shop where the waitresses were dressed like page boys and shepherdesses.

I almost never go down town. I kept saying. "Just think. This goes on all the time."

Anna said, "You are a shut-in. Poor baby."

We were leaving the tea room when she said, "It's easier now, isn't it? You're enjoying this, aren't you?"

I did not need to ask what she meant.

Sometimes at Christmases, walking through a Bargain Town or the Super Warehouse, I have been almost overcome with melancholy at the children, and the women, and the men who fumble in their purses, their pockets, re-count their change, fearful of having to return one of the glittering objects they have selected for someone they had hoped to surprise, or bless.

It has been a long time since I was such a person, forced to leave the sled or the doll or the silver earrings on the counter, making trouble for the check-out girl, apologizing to the manager. But I have had difficulty forgetting that person.

Anna is right. I'm no better shopper than I am a traveler. She's right when she says I have a Depression mind. But she is not unsympathetic. I am sure she understands the difficulty of enduring the kindness of gifts: the expectant look of the givers as they wait for you to remove the ribbon and paper, to say, "I've always wanted . . ."

When he was ten Mark gave me a milk stool he had made in woodwork, a splintered circle of board on three legs that refused to hold the circle.

"What I've always wanted," I said, placing my coffee cup on the stool which tipped over, spilling my coffee on to Robert's gift to me, two Audubon prints, turning the robin into a blackbird, the nuthatch into a Rorschach test.

Diving

Robert was livid. "Look what you did. You've ruined Christmas."

Mark grabbed a wad of tissue paper and began rubbing the birds, upsetting his cocoa.

I have not thought of the milk-stool Christmas for a long time. If Anna were going to be reading these pages tonight I would not be remembering now.

Yesterday we bought scarves and gloves and sweaters and books and keycases. The gifts were generously expensive. With Anna I relished our extravagances. I did not see one human being count out his change.

I HAVE put off writing about last night.

After dinner Anna was slow in settling down to read.

Several times she stopped reading, but I had no notion she was upset. I smiled at the ceiling, remembering the September day at Lake Baldwin, without grief.

When she had finished, we were quiet for a minute. Finally I said, "That was a great dive."

Anna said, "It's not a good idea, Arch."

I was slow in hearing her. Sometimes at home the mantel clock strikes and I do not hear it until after the sound stops. But I am always able to reconstruct the time, remembering the sounds I have not listened to.

"What's not a good idea?"

"Reading this way. Every weekend. I'm not going to read any more."

I sat up quickly. "What's the matter with you?"

Anna was looking at me as if I were somebody she had not met for a long time. She herself was looking like her passport picture. I wondered what photographers thought about the passport pictures they produced. "I'm just not going to read any more. It isn't fair to you. Or me, either."

"What are you talking about, for God's sake. It's all your idea."

"I know. And you mustn't stop writing. I'd die if you stopped."

"What in the hell!"

"You're making us all different. I can't stand it." Anna spoke quietly. "I don't need to stand it."

I was across the room. Anna stood. I was holding her shoulders. "Jesus, Anna. Listen to me. Look at me." I was shaking her shoulders.

"Let go of me. Get your hands off me."

Anna's bones were hard in my hands.

"You're hurting me, Arch. Stop it." Anna was shouting.

I loosened my hands.

Anna slapped me. The sound of her hand on my cheek was loud in the room.

I feel sure she was as surprised as I was. She lifted her hand again. She patted my cheek. Three times she patted my cheek.

She backed away from me. She backed clear to the wall of bookcases.

Two roaches moved on the books above her head. Despite expensive exterminators who visit us every month, we have roaches in our new house. I cannot abide the memory of roaches. Their presence in a house which is only a year old is not to be borne.

I grabbed the pages of the story about Mark from the chair where Anna had been sitting. I slashed at the roaches. I beat at the books after the roaches fell to the floor. The face of the passport woman did not move.

I took the pages, the last page smeared with the bodies of the roaches to the leather wastebasket by my desk. I did not have the energy to crumple the pages. I dropped them into the basket. My hands trembled. I tried to remember my father.

Anna ran her tongue over her lips, as if she had to prime them to speak. "I was furious with you for forgetting to pack the lunch."

"No, you weren't."

"I'd worked hard. I was having my period. Your father had just left. That was the summer he stayed two months. I wanted to have a party Mark wouldn't forget. He did have. I was silly."

"He didn't have time to forget it." I suppose I wanted to hurt Anna. I was hurting myself. "Even if it had been a bad day."

"That night you went to sleep the minute you hit the bed. I wanted to talk about the dive. I knew he was going to die. You make fun of my premonitions, but I had a notion he was going to die."

"Come off it, Anna."

"That night . . . I thought maybe we could get ready for it. Talk about it. It was a terrible night, Arch."

"My God."

"I loved Mark more than the others. I know it's terrible to say. I used to think God would punish me. But I haven't been punished, not really. I have a feeling I won't be now, at least not for loving Mark too much."

I held tightly to the edge of the desk.

"I don't like the way you lie, Arch. You're making things pretty. That was his last birthday. All you remember is the dive. You'll make his funeral pretty. And the days after. You don't remember the way things really were."

"God damn it, Anna."

"It's like practicing death, after it's all over. Don't you know what I mean?"

"I have no notion in God's world."

"You've got to write it, but I don't have to read it." Anna was moving toward me. "Some days I think you and I love each other too much. But I don't have any premonitions about us, not any of those premonitions."

Our arms were around each other. Anna dug her fingernails into my back. "Anna, Anna."

Anna pulled away. "Your poor face." She patted my face. "I'm sorry."

I said, "I'm sorry." I imagined myself standing at the door, watching the man and the woman. The man and woman had had a scene, more violent than they had ever had in their married lives before. Still, it was a very small scene. I felt only drained. Embalmed is a better word.

Anna said, "I want to read it all some time, whatever it is, whatever it turns out to be."

I said, "Tomorrow's another day," echoing myself, and Father, and the dim voice of my mother.

Anna said, "We remember what we can remember. I didn't mean you don't remember."

I said, "You're tired. We're both tired."

Anna said, "I'll take a bath. I'm a touch weary, as your father used to say."

I reached down to take the pages from the wastebasket. My back creaked. Anna stood at the door watching me.

"Kiss. Kiss, Arch?"

We kissed. Anna leaned hard against me. We were awkward.

AS I REMEMBER, we stayed at Baldwin Lake until mid-afternoon. We laughed when we discovered that I had forgot the picnic dinner.

At home, as I remember, when Anna began to set the table Mark said,

"This is supposed to be a picnic, Mom. Let's eat on the back porch. You aren't supposed to sit in chairs at a picnic."

As I remember, we sat on the beach towels spread on the concrete floor of the porch. We were ravenous. Mark's funny menu was delicious. We ate every crumb. Anna made more sandwiches. We had cocoa after the Cokes were gone. We all went to bed early.

I remember that Mark said, "I wish I could go on being twelve forever."

Perhaps he did not say that. But I am pretty sure he said, "I wish I could go on being twelve forever." Anyhow he got his wish.

I am not writing for Anna now, not for a long time.